OTHER BOOKS BY MORGAN LOMAX

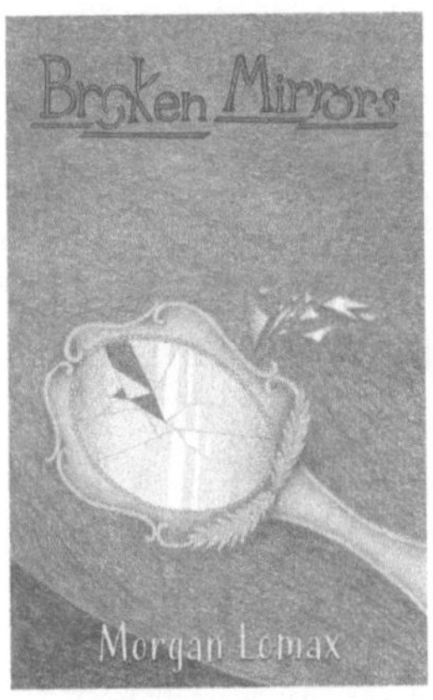

Broken Mirrors

Follow the mysterious doctor, Malchus Marlow, on his miraculous journey of healing and self-discovery in the first two books of the trilogy!

Burning Letters

Burning Letters

Morgan Lomax

Deeds Publishing | Athens

Copyright © 2023 — Morgan Lomax

ALL RIGHTS RESERVED—No part of this book may be reproduced in any form or by any electronic or mechanical means, including information storage and retrieval systems, without permission in writing from the authors, except by a reviewer who may quote brief passages in a review.

Published by Deeds Publishing in Athens, GA
www.deedspublishing.com

Printed in The United States of America

Cover and Illustrations by Morgan Lomax

ISBN 978-1-950794-93-5

Books are available in quantity for promotional or premium use. For information, email info@deedspublishing.com.

First Edition, 2023

10 9 8 7 6 5 4 3 2 1

This book is dedicated first of all to God, without Whom I could not have written it, and to my late Grandpa Lomax, who was a great inspiration for the continuing growth and journey of Master Marlow.

I

The metal door of the mailbox opened with a screech. Master Marlow peered anxiously into its shadowy interior. His heart sank. It was empty. With a sigh, he gently closed the squeaky door, shoved his hands into his pockets, and slowly trekked back toward the house. It was quite convenient having the mailbox right outside the gate instead of at the bottom of the hill. Now, on days when there wasn't any mail, he didn't have to make such long and burdensome trips just to be disappointed.

He glanced up at the fiery sky. The sun was bathing the tips of the trees in golden flames. Such a beautiful sight should have been soothing, but it only made Master Marlow uneasy. It was growing late. Later than normal. He suddenly wished he were wearing a watch. Closing his eyes, he took a deep breath of the crisp evening breeze. The shadows left by the setting sun were already beginning to cool the air for the night. It smelled damp and earthy from the fine layer of leaves blanketing the ground. In the distance, he could hear Felix raking next to the garden. With each stroke, a new wave of crinkled foliage crashed over his swelling mound. A few crickets began tuning their fiddles for their upcoming midnight performance, and the dirt that crunched beneath Master Marlow's feet provided the rattling percussion section. The noise seemed deafening. He slowed his pace. A couple of leaves swirled across his path before somersaulting into the sky. His thoughts drifted along with them.

Fall. A season of constant change. Every day a leaf would yellow a little more around the edges. A tree would grow a little barer, and the wind would blow a little colder. It was a fleeting whirl of color whose only purpose was to make way for winter. Fall was nothing more than a season of decay and death, yet it seemed to mirror the doctor's own life.

Over the past summer, he had been transformed from an almost nonexistent recluse into the benevolent village doctor. Even though his grotesque figure was still marbled with scars and disfigured with a crooked nose and mishappen ears, no one was afraid of him or objected to his presence. In fact, they welcomed him with friendly smiles and warm hearts. It was as if he had always been a part of their little family. No different than anyone else. At first, this unquestioned acceptance relieved him, but now, he was beginning to grow a bit uneasy. So much was changing so quickly. Perhaps a little too quickly. Was the people's kindness genuine and not merely a façade hiding their true feelings? Could he trust them? Or was his dream (like fall) to end in winter's cruel death?

The swift pitter patter of running feet racing up the path behind him jarred him from his thoughts.

"Mr. Marlow!"

The doctor turned just in time to catch Alvera in his arms.

"Alvera." They embraced like two soldiers who had not expected to see each other alive after a war. Master Marlow closed his eyes and smiled. His heart glowed with joy. It had only been a couple of months, but it felt as if he hadn't seen Alvera for years. It comforted him just to be able to hold her in his arms again. Her very presence seemed to chase all his troubles and cares away.

Finally, they released each other.

"I was beginning to think that you weren't coming," he said. Alvera looked bashfully at the ground and dug the toe of one of her shoes into the dirt.

"Sorry. My last class went over today."

"Oh? What class was that?"

"Biology. We're studying amphibians right now. In fact, our teacher said that we would be dissecting a frog next week. I'm really excited about that."

The master chuckled. "I remember when I dissected my first frog. It was fascinating … and hilarious. There was a group of girls in my class that were absolutely terrified of insects, spiders, frogs, snakes, etc. Anyway, that day in biology, the boy next to me wasn't paying attention to what he was doing and let his scalpel slip. It sliced off one of his frog's eyes and sent it flying across the room, and it landed on one of those girls' heads. I'm telling you, Alvera. I don't think I've ever heard anyone scream as loudly as she did."

Alvera giggled.

"Are there girls like that in your class?"

She nodded.

"I don't suppose you're one of them?"

She giggled again. "No!"

"I know you're not. With as much as you love little creatures, you'll enjoy it."

She smiled up at him, and he warmly smiled back. As they stood with nothing more than the whispers of the autumn wind to pierce the serene silence drifting in like a fog around them, the doctor absent-mindedly contemplated his young friend.

He was so proud of her. The past summer and her brief time back in school had really made a difference in her countenance. She was still shy, to be sure, but a new confidence pervaded her every action and word. She was not afraid to stand up for herself and what she believed in, as evidenced by her fashion choice. Delicately draped around her narrow shoulders was the sky-blue cloak he had sewn for her. It rose a bit higher up her calves than it did in the summer, but it still fitted her slender figure nicely. It pleased him greatly to see that she still enjoyed wearing it. Perhaps it made her feel secure and reminded her of him just as the portrait on the mantel did so for the doctor. Aside from these alterations, Alvera was still the same little girl he had found in the woods those few months ago. Her golden hair, though restrained by a hair band, was just as long and flowy as ever. Her cheeks still blushed to the hue of a pale pink rose, and her intensely blue eyes still glowed and glimmered with that tender kindness that had stolen his heart. She was a gentle spirit, and he hoped that she would forever remain so.

His smile broadened after he finished examining her. "You've grown."

She turned her face away as it flushed a deep crimson. To dispel her embarrassment, the master gently patted her on the back. "Come on. You know Felix will want to see you."

Walking side by side, the two friends strolled across the yard and around the left corner of the house. As they went, they resumed their conversation. The only interruptions were the occasional crunches of stray leaves beneath their feet.

"So," began Master Marlow, "how is your first year of high school going?"

"It's going very well. I was nervous at first, but after the first few days, I felt more comfortable with the teachers and the curriculum. I'm enjoying all of my classes. Well … except for algebra."

The doctor looked at her with concern. "Why? Is something wrong? Is the teacher harsh? Is someone bullying you?"

"No, no. It's nothing like that. My teachers are wonderful, and none of the other students have ever been mean to me."

"Then, what is it?"

"I just don't like math."

A sigh of relief escaped the master's lips as an amused smile replaced his worried grimace.

Alvera continued, "I mean … I always do well, but I've always had a hard time with it. And algebra is much more complicated than basic math."

"Don't worry. I'm sure you'll be fine. But if you do have trouble, I'll be more than happy to help."

A sharp gust of wind suddenly darted across their path, driving a herd of leaves before it. Alvera's curious eyes seemed to be swept up in the blast as well. She watched the shriveled crisps tumble and trip clumsily against their wills, for they were completely at the mercy of autumn's chaffing breath. Finally, their irregular progress was stopped by the fence surrounding the garden next to the house. Their frail skeletons rattled against its metal links. However, just as it could not stop the wind, this barricade also could not prevent Alvera's penetrating gaze from pushing through its bars. Inside, she saw the garden itself. It was still just as lush and vibrant as ever, for it was not yet cold enough for winter's frost to crush the silken petals or dull the pointed leaves. However, it was missing the abundance of bees and other insects that usually hovered around its sweet nectars and fragrances. Most of them had probably already tucked themselves away in a cozy corner with plenty of provisions for the coming winter.

As her thoughts shifted back to Master Marlow, she remembered a burning question that she had been meaning to ask him in one of her letters.

"Mr. Marlow?"

The master started a bit before jerking his head in Alvera's direction as if he too had been lost in thought. "Yes?"

"I just remembered. You told me that you accepted the offer to become the village doctor. How is that going?"

He paused a moment, took a deep breath, and exhaled before answering, "Well, to be honest…when I first accepted the job, I thought I had gone mad. In the first place, I had not been a practicing physician in over twenty years, and secondly, I still wasn't entirely comfortable with the idea of being out in public again. But when I went into the village to inspect the building that was to be my facility, I received the warmest welcome. The people were so excited to see me. In fact, they were so friendly, I was a bit startled.

"Soon after, the clinic was up and running, and every single person in the village wanted me as their doctor. It felt good to be trusted and accepted. I never thought I would experience that feeling again. Even though it has been a couple of months since the clinic opened, I still have patients expressing their gratitude for my taking the position." He sighed. "I had forgotten just how much I loved caring for others. I'm glad to be back at it again."

He glanced lovingly at Alvera. "Of course, I never would have considered it if it weren't for you, Alvera. You showed me that the world has changed. Not everyone judges by appearances anymore, and I am very thankful that they don't. I could not have done this without you. Or Mr. Pete! After all, he's the one who mentioned the job to me and helped to get the building for my practice. There are still benevolent people in this world."

A contemplative silence settled around them, but Master Marlow did not linger long in its ensnaring mist. He broke the reverie by looking forward and addressing Alvera.

"I'll have to take you to the clinic and show you around some time. And maybe after hours or on the weekends we could use one of the examination rooms to continue your medical training. Would you like that?"

"Oh, yes! Very much so."

"Now, where did we leave off?" he wondered, grabbing his chin and absentmindedly rubbing its wart-like mole.

"I believe we stopped after the instruments and their uses and how to care for different types of wounds."

"That's right. So next time, I'll begin teaching you about various diseases and their treatments."

Their conversation ended as they stopped just a few feet in front of the busy butler. His small mound of leaves had now grown into a monstrous mountain that the wind threatened to topple at any second. It looked as if Felix had gathered all the leaves from every yard in the entire village, yet more and more continued to appear. Completely oblivious to his audience, he muttered as he furiously raked up the new intruders.

"Look, you! I've raked this spot three times already! If you're going to fall, at least have the decency to fall on the pile."

The wind responded by sending a shower of leaves that landed on and all around the flustered butler. Planting his rake firmly in the ground with one hand, Felix placed his other hand on his hip and gave an exasperated sigh.

"Oh, now you're just mocking me. Where do all of you come from anyway? Ugh! Sometimes I wonder why I even bother raking at all."

Seeing that Felix was far too distracted to notice them, Master Marlow loudly cleared his throat to get his attention. The poor butler was so startled by the sudden noise that he nearly jumped out of his trousers in fright!

"Oh! Master Marlow, Sir. I'm sorry. I didn't see you there. Did you need …" His voice trailed away upon seeing Alvera standing bashfully beside the master. She smiled at him, and an overwhelming joy flooded his entire being. She was back. He couldn't believe it. She was finally back.

"Alvera!" he cried. He started to run toward her, but in his excitement, his left foot caught on the rake, causing him to trip. Before anyone could do or say anything, he went sprawling through the air and belly-flopped onto the pile of leaves. A cascade of brown, crimson, and topaz spilled over the spotless lawn and crashed at Alvera's and Master Marlow's feet. From the midst of the scattered mound, Felix shakily emerged.

What a sight he was! He was covered from head to toe in leaves. They stuck out at odd angles from his wispy hair and beard. They clung to his jacket and waistcoat like leeches, and some had even managed to slip into his mouth. He looked so ridiculous that Alvera couldn't contain her laughter any longer. At first, Master Marlow merely smiled and shook his head, but eventually, even he had to chuckle a bit at the butler's clumsy mishap.

Shaking off as many of the troublesome leaves as he could, Felix waded through the remains of his crumbled pile over to Alvera and wrapped his arms around the still-giggling girl.

"Oh, Alvera! It's so good to see you again! I've missed you so!" He pulled away and held her at arm's length to get a good look at her. "How have you been?"

"Just fine, Mr. Felix. How have you been?"

"I've been doing very well myself. Thank you. As you can see, I've been raking up the leaves. Well … *trying* to. And I still keep busy cleaning, cooking, and gardening as always. Of course, I won't be gardening for much longer now. Winter will be here before we know it. It already seems to be getting chillier by the day. Oh!" he suddenly exclaimed. "Has Master Marlow shown you the house yet?"

She shook her head.

"Well! don't let me detain you any longer. We can save all the cordialities for later. You must see what we've done with the place! Go on! Go on!"

"Wait," she said, interrupting his unbridled enthusiasm. "Do you need any help before we go?"

Felix turned to look at the sea of leaves stretched out behind him that Alvera had indicated. He smiled to himself with deep emotion. Oh, what a kind and compassionate heart she truly had! Facing her again, he gently answered, "No, that's all right. I've got it. There was no way I was ever going to get all those leaves raked up anyway. Go on. I'll catch up with you later."

As the faithful gardener trudged back through the burgundy mass to at least try to tame it, a shrill whinny soared through the air. Surprised and a bit alarmed, Alvera jerked her head toward Master Marlow and stared at him with wide, wondering eyes.

"What was that?"

His ebony eyes glimmered. "I'll show you."

He led the way around the house with Alvera eagerly trotting behind. When they reached the backyard, she saw that a wooden fence now surrounded a fourth of it. At the far end of the enclosure, next to the woods, was a handsome stable fitted with two stalls. Both were freshly strewn with hay and equipped with troughs full of grain and water. Off to the side, two shiny leather saddles and bridles hung from hooks mounted to a beam of the stable.

However, this was not the grandest part of the enclosure. From the middle, two horses came trotting up to their admirers. The faster of the two was a sleek black stallion with a silky mane that gracefully bounced with every movement. His rich coat glittered in the golden rays of the setting sun. Sharply defined muscles rippled from his sturdy neck, slender legs, and ample withers. His pointed ears were perky and constantly on alert, and his flared nostrils quivered with excitement. Intelligence shone in his bright black eyes that rather resembled beads. He was quite an intimidating figure who seemed to inspire more dread and reverence than even the most renowned dignitary. However, this bold armor was softened by a white star that glowed in the middle of his forehead, and it revealed a gentler and more loyal nature that resided deep within him.

The other was also a stallion, but he was solid gray from his tufty mane down to his calloused hooves. The blacks of each of his eyes were rimmed by a pale blue crescent that was partly obscured by lazy eyelids. In fact, his whole demeanor was tinged with laziness as he purposefully lagged behind his companion. However, this flaw revealed his true virtue: an extremely gentle nature. He might not be the swiftest or the most spirited horse, but he was one that could always be trusted to be there by his master's side with tender affections.

"They're beautiful!" Alvera remarked as the two gorgeous creatures hung their heads over the fence. "What are their names?"

"That is Obsidian," he said pointing to the black stallion, "or Sid for short, and the other one is Frank. You can guess whose horse is whose."

For a few minutes, Alvera simply gazed in awe at Obsidian and Frank. It had been a long time since she had seen a horse up close. When her captivation finally lessened, she looked imploringly at Master Marlow. She did not have to say anything for the master to understand. With a knowing smile, he nodded his consent, and Alvera immediately turned back to the horses. After letting him smell her hand, she slowly reached up and began to gently stroke the coal black steed.

"Hello, Obsidian."

The peach fuzz of his muzzle was as soft as velvet. She giggled as the breath from his nostrils tickled the hairs on her arm. It was warm and steamy against the cool evening air and smelled of grass and dried hay.

While she amused herself thus, Master Marlow rambled on: "I bought the horses to use as transportation. I felt bad always having to send Felix on foot to run errands in the village, and it just wasn't feasible for me to walk to work. Especially if I received a house call. Felix suggested to simply buy a car, but that was out of the question. I've never been fond of automobiles or technology in general for that matter. It just doesn't seem completely reliable or consistent to me. Come to think of it, I don't even know if Felix knows how to drive a car."

He pondered for a moment. "I suppose I just prefer the simpler, more traditional ways of life. Either that or I'm just getting old. But the horses also make wonderful companions. I often like to go for a ride or come out here and read. On those occasions, Obsidian will usually lay behind me on the other side of the fence or look over my shoulder and nuzzle my hair. Sometimes, I even talk to him." A rosy flush flared up in his cheeks. "I know it's silly…but I feel like I can tell him anything. All my cares, fears, sorrows, and joys without him judging me."

"It's not silly," Alvera interrupted. "I talk to my pets all the time. They're excellent listeners." She ruffled the top of Frank's mane. "Besides, I find that it's much easier to talk to animals than to people most of the time."

The doctor silently agreed with her.

"Hullo!" shouted a familiar voice.

Both Alvera and Master Marlow turned to see a cheerful Mr. Pete. He sat tottering at the top of an ancient carriage that was pulled by an even more ancient-looking chestnut horse. He was dressed in a dapper black suit with a matching bow tie. A long black cape fluttered like a pair of raven wings behind him, and a spiffy top hat covered in igneous silk bobbled from side to side on his bushy brown curls. Letting go of the reins and spreading his pudgy arms wide, he addressed his audience.

"Hey, Mal! How do I look?"

"Exceptionally sharp," Master Marlow declared.

"Sharp? This?" he asked pointing to his ruddy face. "Why, my beard alone could blunt at least ten razors!" His rotund belly shook violently as a hearty guffaw rumbled forth from his throat. All Master Marlow could do was smile, cross his arms, and shake his head at Pete's absurdity. *What a crazy little man*, he thought, not unkindly to himself.

When he finally pulled the carriage to a stop in front of them, Mr. Pete grabbed a cane that had been lying at his feet and unceremoniously slid from his perch to the ground. With a flourish of his top hat, he took a sweeping bow. He certainly knew how to make an entrance, and no matter how ridiculous he might appear, he held himself with all the pomp and charm of the most dazzling peacock in the world. Replacing his hat back on his head, he strode over to the doctor and clasped his hand in a firm handshake.

"Good to see ya again, Malchus! How've ya been?"

"I've been doing very well, Pete. And yourself?"

"Doin' just dandy! Just dandy! Business is slow as usual, but I've been gettin' a lot more customers thanks to you. Say! How's the doctor business goin'?"

"It's absolutely wonderful. I can't thank you enough for suggesting the position to me and helping me get established."

"Oh, pish posh!" he said with a wave of his chubby hand. "I've told you before. It's not about me. Don't even think of me! It's *you* who this village is indebted to. You're savin' countless lives through your services. And we all greatly appreciate you for it."

Master Marlow didn't know what to say. He had no idea that he meant so much to the little village. All he could do was smile gratefully at his stout friend. Thankfully, Pete didn't notice the doctor's inability to express his feelings, for his attention was suddenly drawn to Alvera who had been silently standing by, contemplatively taking in every word.

"Well, now. Look who we have here! Now, don't tell me. Don't tell me. Is it…Alvera?"

She nodded.

"I knew it! I rarely ever forget anyone who comes into my shop," he said elbowing her. "Probably because there aren't that many to remember!" He laughed at his own witty remark. When his amusement subsided, he looked Alvera up and down. "Blimey! It's been a while since I've seen ya. But it's always a pleasure nonetheless." He took her slender hand and reverentially kissed it. Such an act was received with girlish giggles from the little lady.

Taking his leave, he walked back to his horse and began unhitching him from the carriage. "Well, here's your carriage. All paid and accounted for."

"Thank you, Pete. It's perfect."

"Isn't she?" he concurred, slapping the side door. "She's still got 'er original stain. White oak and burnished cherry. Might need a little bit of touchin' up, but other than that, it's still in good condition. And the carvings on the doors, hood, and wheels are part of the original design too. Yes, sir. Ya won't find a better one than her, and you'd be even more hard pressed to find one that still runs as good as she does at her age. With all her vintage parts too, I might add. She's a little clanky at times, but overall, she'll give you a pretty smooth ride. I never thought I'd be rid of it."

"Well, it's off your hands now," Master Marlow broke in. "It truly is a fine carriage."

"She sure is. And I know she'll be well loved and taken care of here. In fact, I don't think I would've been comfortable sellin' her to anyone but you."

Silence fell as the two men stood admiring the antique craftmanship gleaming before them in the sunlight. However, it couldn't last long with Mr. Pete being present. He took a deep breath, put his hands on his hips, poked out his belly, and sighed.

"Well, I guess I'd better be on my way." He sauntered over to his horse and mounted. The poor creature's back and knees sagged and buckled under the weight. However, he seemed to bear his master considerably well. With a click of the tongue and a sharp kick in the sides, Pete had his horse cantering off. Master Marlow and Alvera waved as he sped away.

"Goodbye, Pete," called the doctor, "and thank you again."

"No problem. Oh! and thanks for the new suit!"

"Any time, Pete. Any time."

"And, Alvera!" he cried before disappearing over the hill. "Don't be such a stranger!" He broke into a chorus of laughter that echoed over the countryside long after he had vanished from sight.

Master Marlow turned to Alvera. "Well, are you ready to see the house?"

She nodded excitedly.

"Follow me."

2

The two friends made their way back around to the front of the house and climbed up the steps to the porch. Holding the front door open, Master Marlow motioned for Alvera to go in first. She was surprised as soon as she crossed the threshold, for mounted on the left wall of the compact foyer was a small oval mirror. It was the first mirror she had ever seen openly displayed in the master's house. As she timidly crept further in, she noticed that the entire house did not seem quite as dark and shadowy as it had before. And, indeed, it was not. Every centimeter of that horrid, purple-veined black wallpaper had been stripped from the walls and was now replaced by a flawless coat of cobalt blue paint. The chairs before the fireplace had been refurbished with navy blue fabric, and the oval rug stationed at their feet sported a striking pattern of rings dyed various shades of blue.

Lining the stairs and upper hall was a new stretch of carpet. Its edges bore a navy trim dotted with flowers while its middle resembled a pool of sky-blue water crossed over and over again with darker lines that created a pattern of diamond tiles on its surface. Every window was framed with striped curtains. This may not seem like a drastic change, but Alvera noticed some details concerning the curtains and widows that certainly were. Not only were the curtains new, but they were also completely pushed off to the sides. The blinds were also thrown wide open to let as much sunlight in as possible. The last time she had been here, every window was locked, barred, and heavily curtained. Hardly any light could penetrate them, and the house seemed stifled and dull. Now, it could breathe freely again and bring new light and life to its inhabitants.

Eventually, she found herself in front of the fireplace and gazed up at the picture the doctor had carefully placed there. She smiled as she looked at the three of them standing together. Master Marlow watched her every movement and burst of amazement with contentment.

With hands clasped behind his back, he stepped forward into the middle of the den. "So…what do you think?"

Alvera jerked her head away from the precious photo. She had almost forgotten that the doctor was still there. Waking from her wonder and daydreams, she replied, "It's beautiful!"

"Thank you," he said slightly blushing. "I picked out the palette. I did some research and found that blue and green are the most soothing colors. With all the changes occurring lately, I figured it would be beneficial for me and Felix to have a calming atmosphere to retreat to." As if to change the subject, he quickly pointed toward one of the windows. "Felix made the curtains."

"They're very nice."

"And did you notice this?" Alvera followed him as he hastily strode into the hallway. He stopped next to a little black box with a spring-like cord mounted to the wall.

"A telephone?"

"Since I resumed work as a full-time doctor, I realized that I might need a more convenient way than the post office for my patients to contact me. If there's an emergency, a house call, or I'm not at the clinic, they can just call my home phone number instead of the business number."

Master Marlow's countenance seemed to falter in the brief pause that followed. It was no more than a flicker, but Alvera saw it. Something was wrong. However, it quickly brightened again. "Come on," he said. "I'll show you the rest of the house."

The operation room was still the same, except for a small incubator that sat on the counter. Master Marlow said he got it to store his bacteria specimens that he used for further studies. Across the hall was the library. It had been painted a forest green, and when they ventured upstairs, Alvera found that the subsequent rooms had also been painted the same color. After viewing the last bedroom of the upper hall, the doctor marched back to the bathroom and opened the door.

"Look inside," he said.

Alvera peeked her head cautiously around the doorframe. At first, there didn't seem to be anything out of the ordinary. Same pale green tile. Same spruce shower, curtains, and rug. Same pedestal sink. However, there was one thing that had changed. As soon as she spotted it, she eagerly turned back to the doctor with a huge grin.

"There's a mirror!"

"Yes. And I can't tell you how elated Felix was when I hung it up. I don't suppose he ever told you about his struggles in the water bowl?"

"He did," she replied with a suppressed giggle.

Master Marlow found himself able to laugh a bit at this joke as well. "Now," he resumed in a more serious tone, "there is one more thing that I want to show you. But…you have to close your eyes."

She was a bit confused at first, but she willingly obeyed the master's request, nonetheless. Her other senses instantly heightened out of unrestrained curiosity. A sharp click struck her ears. It sounded as if a lock were being undone. A haunting creak moaned through the air like the desperate squeak of an injured mouse. It must have emanated from the slow opening of a door. She could hear and feel muffled thumps pacing away from her. Suddenly, Master Marlow's deep voice resonated from some distance away.

"Now, walk straight ahead. Follow the sound of my voice."

Tentatively placing one foot in front of the other, she slowly progressed toward the doctor (she hoped).

"That's it," he encouraged. "Keep going. A little more. A little more. One more step…stop! Stay right there."

A soft boom rumbled behind her.

"All right," he said. "Open your eyes."

Alvera blinked a few times in the blinding light that met her eyes, but once they adjusted to the ethereal atmosphere, she marveled at what she saw. From a solitary window in front of her, golden sunlight streamed into the compact room and caused the gorgeous wood floor to glow like amber. The walls were painted in misty azure. At the top near the ceiling, a narrow trim of wallpaper painted with galloping horses ran around the room. Her wondering eyes wandered back toward the window. Just a little distance in front of it sat a sturdy oak desk and chair. They seemed to be shrouded in billowy clouds which were the curtains draped around the window. As if drawn in by their mystical haze, Alvera slowly drifted toward them.

"Wow!" she breathed as she rounded the desk. Reaching out a slender hand, she playfully batted at the wispy drapery as if to determine if it were really tangible or not. Suddenly, she froze. There was something vaguely familiar about this place. After a moment of contemplation, she turned to face the master. "Is this the forbidden room?"

"Yes. Well, it was."

"I didn't know there was a window in here."

"You couldn't have. It was always covered by those mirrors. Remember? I had quite forgotten about it myself. I had also forgotten just how bright it made this little room." He looked around, lost in thoughtful reflection until his gaze settled back on Alvera. "Do you like it?"

"I love it! In fact, I think this might be my new favorite room of the house."

"I'm glad to hear that because … it's for you."

She gave him a confused look. Had she heard him correctly? The doctor could see the questions multiplying and buzzing in the aqua waters of her eyes.

"I turned this room into a little study for you," he explained. "That way, whenever you come over after school, you'll have a quiet place of your own to work on homework."

She stood motionless for a moment as if she didn't know how to respond before dashing across the room and throwing her arms around the startled doctor.

"Thank you, Mr. Marlow! But…you didn't have to do this."

"I wanted to," he said relaxing a bit. "Besides…I needed to remodel this room. More so than any of the others."

To Alvera's surprise, he abruptly pulled away from her and coldly turned toward the door. "However, as you can see, I still haven't been able to bring myself to hang these portraits throughout the house. I…I guess I…just don't know what to do with them."

He walked gravely with his hands clasped behind him, and his back seemed to stoop a bit more than it usually did. Alvera's suspicions were confirmed. She *had* noticed a subtle alteration in his mood. Something was definitely troubling him.

So as not to disturb his thoughts, she quietly moved up beside him and joined his upward gaze. Dozens of bland faces greeted her with indifferent glances. They seemed even more forbidding than the first time she had encountered them, and their intense looks of condemnation and disdain cast an oppressive shadow over the front half of the room. This shadow was an iron cloak that fettered Master Marlow. She could see its weight physically pulling him down. Her eyes wandered to an oval portrait of a particularly ill-tempered looking man. His coal-hard eyes pelted her with such a frigid stare that a shiver shot up her spine. She instinctively turned away. Alvera didn't blame the master for not feeling ready to display his family's portraits throughout the house. She couldn't imagine having to endure such contemptible gazes boring into her back and head no matter what room she was in.

Venturing another peek, she glanced back up at the collage of pictures. This time, her eyes rested on an elongated oval frame containing a black and white picture of a young woman. She had long, straight hair that appeared to be as brittle as straw left to dry in the sun for too long. Her skin was thinly stretched over her narrow bones, and dark bags sank just above her cheeks, causing her gray eyes to appear to be too large for her head. However, there was something in those eyes that captivated Alvera. Despite their obvious fright and fatigue, they were kind and gentle. She was different from the rest. Perhaps she was an outcast just like Master Marlow. Her thoughts drifted back to what the master had told her about his family. How they had mistreated him. How they blamed him for ruining their legacy. How he had left at such a young age. Nothing had ever been resolved.

A light suddenly illuminated her jumbled thoughts. She understood. In subdued tones, she gently broke the uncomfortable silence. "You've been thinking about them a lot lately. Haven't you?"

Without diverting his gaze, the master solemnly nodded. He looked as if he wanted to speak, but the words wouldn't come. Silence reined again. Finally, he found his voice and took a deep breath.

"I just…I wish I could settle things with them. Make

amends. But … at the same time … I'm afraid. I just don't know if I'm ready."

"I understand. You don't have to confront your whole family at once. That would be a lot to ask. Besides, you've already improved so much. But … if you could talk to one of them … who would it be?"

"My mother. Definitely," he said, looking directly at the portrait of the woman with the gentle eyes. Alvera nodded. She remembered the special bond the master had shared with his mother. She was the only person in his family who had ever cared about him. She also remembered how he had left her without saying goodbye. Oh, how he regretted that! If it were possible, the master would do anything to make it right.

She turned and looked at him. "Then why don't you?"

For the first time since he had walked over to the cluster of pictures, Master Marlow pulled his gaze away from them and looked at Alvera. Her wide eyes were burning with hope as she expectantly waited for an answer. The doctor mulled over her question. For some reason, it had never occurred to him to go to his mother in person. He brightened at the idea, but his countenance quickly dimmed as his melancholy cloud drifted back over him. It was a simple plan, yet it had its complications.

"I would," he began, "but … it's been so long. I don't know if she lives in the same house or if she's even still alive."

"You won't know unless you try."

Master Marlow turned away to consider the matter. While he pondered, he nervously fidgeted with his hands.

Unable to figure out what to do with them or his situation, he eventually shoved his hands in his pockets and stared at the floor.

"I…I don't know. So many things have been changing here lately. I just don't know if I'm ready…or…if I can handle any more changes."

"You can," she said resting a hand on his arm. "I know it. And, if it makes you feel any better, I can come with you."

Master Marlow thought about the proposal and chuckled. He patted Alvera on the back and smiled. "Dear Alvera. What would I ever do without you?"

She sheepishly grinned back at him.

"Well, you better call your parents and ask them if you can go. We'll leave first thing tomorrow morning."

With a surge of excitement, she ran out the door and down the stairs. As soon as she was gone, the master's smile faded. He turned toward the window. The sun had finally sunk below the horizon, leaving streaks of pink and lavender across the royal blue sky. Night was quickly approaching, which meant that tomorrow was not far behind. Tomorrow. Tomorrow was Saturday, and he never worked on the weekends.

Well, I guess I don't have an excuse for not going, he thought. Perhaps it was for the best, for if he delayed the trip, it would only give him more opportunities to change his mind. This was something he needed to do. Something he had wanted to do. But the more he thought about it, the more anxious he became. He had not seen any of his family for more than twenty years. What did tomorrow hold for him? What would he find? If his mother were still alive and well, what would he say to her? How would he even approach the subject he wished to discuss with her? And if it turned out that she had already passed away, what would happen then? How would the master handle such news? Would he be able to live with all the wounds and regrets that would have no more chance of being resolved? Whether he was ready or not, he would find out tomorrow.

3

The delicate fragrances of dew, clover, and leaves floated in through the carriage windows on the breath of the crisp morning mist. Alvera shivered and pulled the folds of her cloak more tightly around her shoulders. They were on their way. And Master Marlow had not been joking when he said that they would leave first thing in the morning, for just before sunrise, Felix had hitched up the horses, driven to the end of the driveway, and turned onto the main road. Now, they were leisurely rolling along a beautiful countryside illuminated by the first pale rays of the sun to peek over the tops of the trees. The entire terrain was a composite of lush green hills that burrowed into the earth like clusters of sleeping turtles. Here and there, a stray shrub or tree protruded from one of their backs, and a few of them bore the stripes of tractors that had recently harvested them for their hay.

On either side of this landscape, dense groves of pine trees interspersed with hardwoods rose like castle walls to seal it off from the rest of the world. This created a sense of security and peace. In fact, it was so quiet and serene that Alvera wondered if they were the only living things passing through this part of the country. The only sounds she could hear were the rhythmic clopping of the horses' hooves against the dirt road, soft creaks and groans from the boards of the carriage as it bounced and jolted along, and the merry twitters of songbirds flitting among the trees.

The carriage seemed to sway to the beat of the harmonious melody of nature, and it threatened to lull Alvera back to sleep. However, her concern for the master allowed her to resist the temptation. Straightening in her seat, she glanced over at his rigid figure. He could have passed for a statue. He simply sat there stiff-backed with his head facing resolutely forward. His scarred face was frozen in an impassive cast, and his eyes blankly stared into the wooden panel of the carriage in front of him. However, it was not the panel that they saw. Whatever it was, it was something distant and invisible to the rest of the world. The only sign that he was still alive was the occasional blinking of his eyelids. Alvera shifted her gaze and noticed the master's attire. He was wearing his black cloak today. That could only mean one thing; he was incredibly uncomfortable. She understood. This was a huge step for him. A difficult step. And who knew where it would lead him?

A quivering motion suddenly caught her attention. She followed it down to the master's lap where his hands were nervously fiddling with the edges of his cloak. The sight caused her sensitive heart to ache. Reaching out her right hand, she tenderly placed it on the doctor's own hands in an attempt to steady them. Their twitching instantly stopped under the gentle pressure, and Master Marlow looked down to see what it was. When he realized that it was Alvera, he turned toward her. They looked earnestly into each other's eyes. Even though his seemingly impenetrable exterior hid his emotions well, his midnight orbs could not hide them from her. In fact, they seemed to long to tell her what his lips could not express at the moment.

He was clearly filled with countless trepidations along with other feelings that she couldn't quite identify. Undoubtedly, they must be caused by the unpleasant memories that this journey had resurfaced. She attempted a reassuring smile. Her eyes glowed with the compassion that was welling up from her heart. Master Marlow knew that she was just trying to comfort him, but she didn't have to try so hard. Just knowing that she was right beside him soothed his tumultuous emotions and gave him courage. Placing a hand on top of hers, he returned an equally reassuring smile as if to say, "It's all right. I'm fine. Thank you for checking on me."

Soon, the tranquil countryside transitioned to a bustling town. Even though it was still quite early in the morning, the streets were already swarming with activity. Countless pedestrians dressed in dapper suits and trench coats scurried along the sidewalks. Some were heading to work, and others were simply passing the time darting in and out of the various shops and cafés that lined the streets. Cars greedily scrambled for parking, and the drivers honked angrily at anyone who got in their way. Taxies zig zagged through the traffic and crowds so impatiently that they nearly flattened a few unsuspecting bystanders in the process.

This was nothing like the little village back home. It was crowded, noisy, uninviting, and rather frightening. However, it was not without some admirable qualities. For such a large and prodigious town, Alvera was surprised at how clean it was. She had always heard that urban areas were susceptible to being littered with garbage and intoxicated with pollution. However, not a speck of grime could be seen in the widest square or the narrowest alley, and the air was reasonably clear. Even the buildings were well maintained. None of the paint seemed faded or chipped, and no cracks could be discerned in any of the walls or foundations. If the town had been one hundred years old, no one would have been able to guess it.

Alvera also appreciated its design. Every building from the town hall to the tiniest tea shop was constructed in Victorian style. It created a sort of unity almost akin to the familial bond felt back in the village. It was strangely enjoyable and elegant. In fact, it was so aesthetically pleasing that the town looked as if it belonged in a painting that captured equally meticulous details.

A light tapping on her shoulder pulled her attention away from the window. Master Marlow met her gaze.

"This is where I grew up."

Leaning on its sill, she looked back out the window and tried to envision a younger Master Marlow tottering along the sidewalk with his family. Perhaps he had once stopped to peer into the window of the sweet shop. Or maybe as he walked, he had swatted at the low-hanging branches of the trees that lined the road. After a moment of such daydreams, she pulled herself back into the carriage and turned toward the master. An anxious excitement electrified her eyes.

"Does that mean we're almost there?"

"Yes," he replied with a nod. "Almost."

After winding through several more crowded streets, Master Marlow, Alvera, and Felix finally rolled out into the country once again. On this side of the town, the hills were clothed in a gold and amber patchwork quilt of trees that cast the road in perpetually shifting shadows. Small portions of the vibrant tapestry were cut out to make room for houses scattered here and there. They reminded Alvera of little groundhogs timidly poking their furry heads out of their burrows. Felix guided Obsidian and Frank down multiple roads arranged in this manner. Each one revealed another section of woods dotted with homes. It was a labyrinth that did not seem to have an end. Did they even know where they were going?

The carriage suddenly slowed and turned sharply to the right. Gravel crunched noisily beneath its wheels. Just as they emerged from the shadows covering the road, Alvera stuck her head out of the window to get a better view. The intense sunlight blinded her for a moment, but once her eyes adjusted to its glare, she beheld the most charming little house she had ever seen. It was built with wooden panels just like the master's house, but it was painted solid white. The middle extended inward slightly to create an awning for a door. Baskets of pink, purple, and white flowers lined the entrance, and emerald-green bushes grew in a row against the house. There were no windows, so to break up the monotony of the white panels, long strands of ivy had been permitted to grow up the wall on either side of the door. To the left was the front porch, equipped with rocking chairs and other furniture. On the right, a white Lincoln town car was parked beneath a flimsy-looking metal carport. A brick chimney rose up from the gray roof. Around three sides of the property, a slim margin of woods enclosed the house and allowed some privacy from the neighbors. It was so beautiful and peaceful, yet a strange uneasiness seemed to distort the cheery guild of the place.

As soon as the carriage grumbled to a stop, Master Marlow quickly hopped out, followed by Alvera. He turned to Felix.

"Thank you, Felix. I'll call when I'm ready for you to come pick us up."

"Very good, Sir," he replied with a nod. Snapping the reins and clicking his tongue, he started the horses back down the driveway. "Have fun!"

The master grimaced at the word. Fun. He had a feeling that this visit was going to be anything *but* fun.

4

As soon as the carriage disappeared from sight, Master Marlow turned without a word and slowly advanced toward the house. Alvera silently trailed behind. The master's feet felt as if they had suddenly been transformed into two lead blocks. They dragged over the miniscule pebbles of gravel as if each piece were a monstrous boulder. He walked like a man being led to his execution. Every fiber of his body resisted the momentum propelling him toward his doom, but his heart urged him on. It was the right thing to do. He would not feel better until he knew.

However, the closer he got to the door, the more unsure he became. His eyes darted nervously from one end of the house to the other. Nothing was familiar. He did not remember the house ever being painted white, and ivy had certainly never been allowed to grow up the sides in such an unruly manner. It took all his courage to resist the urge to pull up his hood.

When he was about a foot away from the door, he stopped. A mat lay just before his feet. It had the word "WELCOME" stamped in black across its shaggy surface.

The master certainly didn't feel welcome. He felt as if he were an intruder invading an enemy country. Reluctantly, he forced himself to look at the door. The palms of his hands and the soles of his feet began to sweat profusely. His heart sounded like a herd of wild horses stampeding in his chest. A sickening dizziness swept over him, and his vision blurred. Even though a flood of adrenaline threatened to send him rocketing into space, he could not move. He just stood there paralyzed by terror. Meanwhile, his mind reeled from one panicked question to the next. *What if it's not her? What if this was a mistake? Why can't I knock? What am I doing?*

After a few more moments of frenzied silence, Master Marlow finally managed to steady his racing thoughts and jittery nerves. If he kept procrastinating and debating with himself, he would end up standing there all day. No more hesitation. He had to act now. Taking a deep breath, he raised his hand toward the doorbell. She couldn't be sure, but Alvera thought she saw the master's hand—perhaps even his entire arm—tremble from the exertion. He pressed the button, and a soft chime resonated inside.

As soon as the last of its piercing note faded away, the world was plunged in a ghostly silence. Alvera strained to hear even the faintest peep, but all was in vain. It was as if time itself had stopped with the stroke of that bell. Nothing happened. Nothing stirred. Every living thing was frozen in its place, and all eyes were glued to the door. It seemed as if the whole world were holding its breath in anxious anticipation. It was leaning toward the fated portal. Waiting for any sign of life. Searching for the slightest movement.

Alvera suddenly jumped, for it sounded as if a cannon had exploded. She tentatively peeked around the edge of the master's cloak. It wasn't a cannon. It was the sound of a bolt being turned in a lock. The door was opening! Time had restarted, but everything seemed to unfold in slow-motion. Both watched in absolute astonishment as the crack in the door slowly grew wider and wider. Who was it? What would they say? When the entrance was just large enough to admit a person, an elderly lady, not much taller than Alvera, scooted out onto the welcome mat. Half of her silver hair was pulled into a messy bun that stuck out like a doorknob from the top of her head. The other half hung in long, straight strands down her back. Two gray eyes that had lost their youthful glow over the years smiled out from the wrinkles that framed them. Gaunt cheeks cast tired shadows up and down her pale face, and her frail frame seemed to be swallowed up by her clothes.

She was dressed in house slippers, tan hose, a white skirt, an oversized gray sweater with lace and beadwork around the collar, and a pale pink shawl draped carelessly around her slender shoulders. She was both an object of benevolence and pity.

Looking up at her visitors, she spoke with a thin yet sweet voice. "Yes? Who is…" She abruptly stopped. A desperate spark brought a new vitality to her eyes as she furiously examined the man standing before her. It was as if she were searching for something. A precious heirloom lost many years ago that she was now on the verge of discovering. Suddenly, she met the master's gaze, and her eyes grew larger than seemed possible. She could not look away;

she was caught in the magnetic pull of those two unsearchable black holes before her.

Involuntarily, her bony hands shakily rose to her face and covered her mouth. She closed her eyes and shook her head. Upon opening them again, they were immediately drawn back to the master's midnight orbs.

"Malchus?" came her tremulous, muffled voice.

The master slightly nodded, and controlling his voice as best he could, he hoarsely whispered, "Hello…Mother."

Her hands dropped to her chest, revealing her gaping mouth. A watery smile soon replaced her shock as her eyes filled with tears. "Oh, Malchus!" She rushed forward and wrapped her arms tightly around him. "My boy! You've come back to me! You've come back!"

Master Marlow tenderly rubbed his mother's back as she sobbed into his shoulder. Closing his eyes, he rested his head against her hair and breathed in its familiar scent. It instantly transported him back to his childhood. There he was—a toddler—being pulled onto his mother's lap. She folded her embracing arms around him. They filled him with warmth and security. Now, she was bending over to kiss him goodnight. Her hair fell in curtains that gently brushed his cheeks and filled the air with their heavenly perfume. It was the fragrance of comfort. A soothing balm for all his wounds. It banished all the evils of the day and made him feel as if nothing could ever harm him again.

But life had made him wiser. No matter how hard he tried, he could never return to such a state of innocent bliss. He was only permitted a fleeting glimpse of it in precious moments such as this one. A flood of emotion sent him sailing back to the present. He struggled to suppress it but managed to keep it under control.

After her overflowing rapture subsided, she released her son and dabbed at the corners of her eyes with her shawl. Her whole face glowed, and a rosiness even seemed to have returned to her cheeks as she beamed up at him. Of course, it could have simply been some redness leftover from crying.

"Look at you," she said inspecting her son. "You've grown into a fine man."

The master attempted to smile, causing his mother's grin to broaden. Suddenly, something else caught her attention. Leaning to the side, she saw for the first time Alvera standing sheepishly behind the master. Her eyes grew wide and glossy again as she looked back at her son in astonishment.

"You have a daughter?"

The master was caught off guard by this question. In fact, it startled and confused him so much that he couldn't give an answer. No matter. His mother was too overjoyed to wait for one.

"After all these years, one of my sons has finally gotten married!"

"Married?" Master Marlow repeated, finally regaining his voice and cognition. "No, no, no, no. I'm not married." He stepped to the side and motioned for Alvera to come forward. "Mother, this is Alvera. She is a very dear friend of mine. In fact, she's *like* a daughter to me, but…no…she's not my biological daughter. Alvera, this is my mother, Agatha Marlow."

For a moment, his mother's cheerful countenance was overshadowed with mild disappointment; however, she quickly recovered. Stepping forward, she grasped one of Alvera's hands and smiled.

"Hello, Alvera. It's a pleasure to meet you."

"It's a pleasure to meet you as well, Mrs. Marlow."

"My!" she exclaimed laughingly, "such fine manners! That's hard to come by in youth nowadays." A brief silence ensued while Mrs. Marlow admired her young visitor and reminisced on those admirable qualities of the past. She was suddenly jarred from her nostalgic thoughts by the remembrance of where she was and what she was doing. "Oh! I'm such a rude hostess! Keeping both of you out here much longer than necessary with trivial chatter and other frivolities. Please, come in! Come in!"

Opening the door, she motioned for them to enter.

Master Marlow paused in the tiny foyer and surveyed his surroundings. Just like the outside, everything inside was completely different. Obviously, his mother had done some remodeling. The cedar boards on the walls were now covered with a flowery wallpaper that seemed to brighten the environment. The wooden floors were cushioned with a plush layer of gray carpet. All the furniture was new, and glass, lace, and other delicate decorations ornamented every table and shelf. There was even a garden just outside the den that could be viewed through sliding glass doors. A garden! His father hated plants. And he certainly would never have allowed such frivolous baubles, senseless doylies, and extravagant designs to deface *his* house.

Master Marlow ventured back to his childhood once again. Back then, the house had always been hollow and bare. Everything was dark, hard, and cold. The master remembered being terrified of the shadows that haunted every room. He never wanted to be left alone with those ghostly phantoms for fear that they would ensnare him and drag him away with their slimy claws. Consequently, he never strayed too far away from his parents or siblings when he was inside. But this was only another form of torment and oppression. Sometimes he wondered if it would be better to be consumed by the monsters than to endure his family's mocking and bullying. It was a constant battle.

They lived in a minimalist environment. Little furniture and even fewer comforts were to be found. Their lifestyle was poorer and much more deplorable than it had to be. His father was by no means rich, but his salary was more than sufficient to provide middle class quality furnishings.

However, his father also kept a tight fist around the neck of the moneybag. He would not spare even the smallest expense to increase his family's pleasure or comfort.

Life was hard, and hard work was the only way to survive. That was something he wanted to engrain in his wife and children. He was a tough, harsh man who wanted a house that would reflect those same rugged qualities, but the house that now lay before the master had been manicured by a feminine touch. He couldn't believe the transformation. Perhaps his father had softened in his old age.

Aside from its makeover, the layout of the house was exactly as he remembered it. The kitchen lay on the right, and the left opened to the den. On the left wall of this room before the sliding doors, another door led to the front porch. Beyond the den, a narrow hallway with four bedrooms branching off extended down the remaining length of the house. It wasn't much, but it still felt like home.

Agatha closed the door with a soft click and shuffled animatedly around her guests. "Boys," she said addressing the den, "you'll never believe who it is!"

The master followed the direction of her voice. His heart froze and fell like a lump of ice into the pit of his stomach. Sitting on one of the pale pink couches covered in a pattern of flowers were his brothers, Andrew and Michael.

"It's your brother, Malchus!"

5

A tense stillness settled over the house as the brothers stared at one another. Michael gawked with gaping mouth and wide eyes; Andrew, on the other hand, clenched his jaw in irritation. He was vexed by his long-lost-brother's return, but for the sake of his mother, he endeavored to conceal his vexation by appearing to be as shocked as Michael was. However, instead of smothering his true feelings, this feigned emotion mixed with them, causing him to appear either highly offended or deeply disgusted.

Master Marlow's face was as impassive as ever, but on the inside, his mind and heart raced from one emotion to the next. He had not expected this. Not one bit. However, the more he thought about it, the more he realized the folly of his fantasies. *You fool! How could you not have foreseen this? You are not her only relative, and she still has your father. What were the odds of finding her alone?* Panic began to set in. *This was a huge mistake. I never should have come.* For a brief, frantic moment, he contemplated bolting for the door. After all, since he wouldn't be able to discuss what he wanted to, there was no point in continuing this uncomfortable visit any longer. His mother stopped him from carrying out this idea.

"Well, go on in! Go on in! I'll be right back. I have some biscuits that I need to put in the oven. Just make yourselves at home!"

Before the master could utter one word in protest, Mrs. Marlow vanished into the kitchen. There was no turning back now. It would be rude and quite unseemly to refuse such open hospitality, and he did not wish to wound his mother any more than he already had. Taking a deep breath, he forced himself to proceed into the den. He felt as if he were being led into an arena to battle two ferocious lions. Who would survive the fight was still uncertain. When he rounded the corner of the sofa opposite his brothers, he hesitated and muttered something that Alvera could not quite make out. It must have been an attempt at friendliness, for Michael eagerly responded with a warm greeting.

Without acknowledging him, Master Marlow anxiously sat down and busied himself by fiddling with the edges of his cloak. Alvera tentatively scooted onto the cushion next to him and pressed herself closely to his side. Michael flashed an encouraging smile at her every time she ventured a glance in his direction, but as soon as she caught his eye, she shyly ducked her head and cowered closer to the master. While the two of them continued their game of cat and mouse, Master Marlow became painfully aware of his being watched as well. Even though he dared not make eye contact or even risk the most furtive of glances, he could feel Andrew's hate-filled eyes burning a hole through the top of his head. Oh! how he wished to be able to disappear at that very moment!

Thankfully, they did not have to remain in that terribly awkward and silent situation for long, even though it felt as if it had already lasted an hour, for Mrs. Marlow promptly returned from the kitchen.

"Sorry for the delay," she said smoothing out her skirt and sitting down next to Alvera. "I know you all must have so much to talk about. Oh! but first…" She shifted toward the rigid girl and placed a bony hand on her shoulder. "I'd like to introduce you to Alvera, Malchus's little friend. Alvera, these are my other two sons. Andrew, the eldest." He solemnly nodded. "And Michael, my youngest."

"Hello, Alvera," Michael said extending his hand. "I'm delighted to meet you."

She was stunned for a moment, but she eventually managed to stammer, "I'm…delighted to meet you as well."

Agatha beamed at how well her company was already getting along, and seeing a perfect object to focus their conversation, she eagerly turned her eyes upon the master.

"Malchus, how did you and Alvera become acquainted in the first place?"

Master Marlow was startled by the sudden question. He had no inclination or even preparation for speaking. In fact, he had hoped to pass most of his time on the couch unseen or as the silent observer. However, this was not to be. After all, it was only natural that *he* should be the center of unwanted attention. All eyes were glued to him, and even in this moment of intense interest, Andrew's venomous stare did not abate. Beads of sweat collected on his forehead. He tried to hide his apparent nervousness by wiping the perspiration over his raven hair.

"Uh…well, I actually just met Alvera over this past summer."

"Really?" interjected his mother.

"Yes. You see…she had been in a plane crash and ended up in the woods around my house. She was severely injured, so I took her in and cared for her."

"Poor thing," Andrew remarked in a barely audible whisper while shaking his head.

Michael gave him a sharp look as if to reprimand such a response before directing his attention back to Malchus. All this went unnoticed by the others.

"Eventually," the master continued, "I was able to get her back to her parents."

"What a remarkable story!" his mother marveled with glowing eyes. "Of all the places in the world, she ended up in the hands of a doctor who had everything she needed."

"Yes, remarkable," Andrew whispered again.

"You know," Agatha said addressing her two other sons, "when they first arrived, I thought that Alvera was Malchus's daughter and that Malchus was married!"

"Malchus, married?" Andrew muttered slightly louder than before with a scoffing laugh. "Not likely."

Someone cleared his throat. Andrew looked over to find Michael glaring at him once again. This time, their subtle actions did not escape everyone's attention. Alvera had noticed their secretive exchange. Were his brothers talking about him? Were they mocking him, calling him horrible names? She quickly stole a glance at Master Marlow to see if he had noticed the strange whispers and looks between his brothers. He was still poised in that same uncomfortably rigid position, and his eyes were still resolutely facing the floor. However, they were not idly roaming over the carpet; the deep recesses of those black waters churned and swirled in agitated contemplation. He had heard and seen it all as well. A pang of compassion and regret suddenly pricked Alvera's heart, causing it to throb painfully with every beat. If only she knew what he was thinking!

Still as oblivious to the surrounding altercations as ever, Mrs. Marlow rambled on with a melancholy sigh. "I had so hoped that one of my sons would marry before I die. But…there is still time." She flashed a mischievous grin at Andrew. "Andrew's been engaged to a young lady in town for quite a while now. It's a wonder they haven't started making plans to be wed yet! I know that if I were…oh! I can never remember her name. What was it, Andrew?"

Andrew abruptly leaned forward and forcefully shook his head at his mother. She simply laughed.

"Oh! he's always so secretive about the whole thing! I don't know why. It's nothing to be ashamed of. For the longest time, he refused to tell us what her name was, and even after that, he's only mentioned it once or twice. We haven't even seen the lucky lady yet! You really must invite her over soon, Andrew. I so look forward to meeting her. After all, if you two are going to spend the rest of your lives together, she must get acquainted with her new family."

After one final warning look from her son, Mrs. Marlow decided to drop the subject.

"All right. All right. I won't embarrass you anymore."

A slight pause ensued before she turned toward the master once again.

"Malchus, you remember Andrew went to school to be a lawyer?"

He nodded.

"Well, he also got a degree in business, and for several years now, he has worked as an accountant at the law firm in town. He's done remarkably well, and everyone who knows him says he's one of the most reliable and efficient accountants they've ever met."

For the first time since his arrival, Master Marlow ventured a glance at his older brother. Their eyes locked. Andrew's chestnut orbs glittered malevolently. A smug grimace of superiority contorted his tightly pressed lips, and the master even fancied that he saw his brother's chest inflate a few centimeters. He hung his head like a dog that had been beaten in a fight. *He hasn't changed a bit*, he thought bitterly to himself. Andrew was still the same prideful, haughty, cruel, and vengeful boy he had always been. If he had not amended his ways after all this time, what were the chances of him doing so in the future? The master was roused from such depressing thoughts by the sound of his mother's voice shimmering through the room once again.

"And Michael says that he still doesn't quite know what he wants to do, but I believe it's because he's more of a Renaissance man than anything else. Everything he puts his hands to he excels at. There's not a job he can't do. In fact, he just started a new job at the post office last week."

"U…uh…Mother," Michael interrupted, coloring a bit. "It's a stationery shop. I started working at a stationery shop."

"Oh, yes! That's right. A stationery shop. The post office was the one before that. Wasn't it?"

Coloring even more, Michael turned his head away, propped it on the back of his left hand, and refused to answer. It was the first time during this entire conversation that he avoided all eye contact. However, this did not faze Mrs. Marlow.

"Malchus," she began, "I assume you're still involved in the medical field?"

"Oh…yes," he said distractedly as he pulled his attention away from Michael. He had to repeat what she said several times in his mind before it made any sense at all. As soon as he comprehended what she was asking, he was instantly filled with confusion. A stark crease forming between his scrunching brows cleft his forehead in two as he cocked his head and examined his mother with suspicious apprehension.

"How did you know I worked in the medical field?"

"Oh…well, from the newspaper of course."

That's right. The paper had featured a few articles on the doctor back when he was a full-time surgeon. Master Marlow cringed at the recollection.

"I remember the first article we ever read about you," continued Mrs. Marlow. "It said that you had become the number one surgeon in the country. I couldn't believe it. We were all so very proud of you."

The master didn't know what to say. Hundreds of emotions tumbled together in the dryer of his mind as he tried to sort through how he felt. Proud? His family was proud of...*him?* He had never heard those words from any of them before, and he almost didn't believe them. However, an unexpected source confirmed them to be true.

"Indeed," agreed Andrew. "In fact, *I* even enjoyed reading about you. One article, in particular, was my absolute favorite. I believe it had the word 'Frankenstein' in the title. Shall I go fetch it and read it to you?"

"Andrew!" Michael whispered rather loudly. His older brother looked at him and mouthed, "What?" as if he failed to understand what he had done to deserve such a quick reprimand. Alvera, on the other hand, understood everything perfectly. She turned to the master to see how he had weathered the blow. He looked gloomier than he had when they had first arrived. She tenderly placed a loving hand on his arm. Andrew shrewdly observed the minutest detail of their actions toward one another.

Pretending not to have noticed the obvious hostility in one of her sons, Agatha hastily addressed the master with a forced air of cheer and tranquility. "So, is your career as a surgeon still going well?"

Master Marlow hesitated to answer. What would he say? That he had given up on humanity, quit his job, and isolated himself from society for twenty years? No. It was a secret that was still too sensitive for him to relate just yet. Carefully selecting his words, the master skirted around the question.

"Well, I'm actually not a...big time surgeon anymore. I recently opened up my own clinic, and I am now the local physician of my village. But I do still perform surgeries when necessary."

"Oh! that's wonderful, Malchus!" his mother remarked. "How are you liking this new position?"

"I enjoy it very much."

"I'm glad."

More awkward silence fell over the room. No one, not even Agatha, seemed willing to pick up the conversation this time. They all simply sat there contained within their own minds. A puzzling thought suddenly entered the master's mind, and before he could stop it, he found himself blurting it out loud.

"Where is Father? How has he been?"

Everyone looked just as surprised as the master did by the suddenness of his question. He instantly regretted his haste. Surely it was not wrong of him to inquire about his father. They had never gotten along or even cared much about each other to be sure, but he still desired his father's well-being. Growing more anxious by the unnaturally prolonged silence, Master Marlow looked impatiently from one family member to the next. They had all (even Andrew!) averted their gazes from him. His anxiety was replaced with a dreadful unease.

Something was wrong. He turned to his mother one last time. Out of the corners of her eyes, she could see her son's yearning eyes pleading for an answer. Their pitiful puppy dog gaze wrenched at her heart. She didn't know what hurt her more, to withhold the truth from her son or to burden him with its terribleness. Whatever she decided, she could not ignore her son any longer. Taking a deep breath, she slowly turned her sorrowful gray eyes back on the master. He instantly searched their watery depths for any sign of information.

"Malchus," she began gravely, "your father is dead. He passed away several years ago."

Her words hit him like an iron door and left him completely numb. His father was dead? Hopelessness billowed like a grievous cumulonimbus cloud in his chest. Now, he would never see him again. He would never have a chance to mend their relationship. True, he had come for the sole purpose of consoling and apologizing to his mother, but he had hoped to eventually connect with his whole family again. Even with his father. But now his dream was gone, and nothing could bring it back. Nothing.

Andrew noticed his brother's festering despair and desired to feed it even more. Turning an evil eye upon him, he muttered, "Yes, how nice of you to finally show an interest in your family after the time we needed you the most is gone."

As if it were an involuntary reflex, Michael whipped his hand across the couch and smacked Andrew on the arm.

"Oww!" he cried rubbing the sting from his assault.

Suddenly, a shrill beeping pierced the air.

"Oh!" cried Mrs. Marlow springing to her feet. "The biscuits. Don't mind me. You boys keep right on talking. I'll be back as soon as I finish making the tea."

She shuffled off to the kitchen. As soon as the last of her skirt slid out of sight, Andrew nearly jumped off the couch and hurriedly stalked out of the room and down the hall. Alvera wondered at his hasty exit. If he had been that eager to leave, she could only imagine how the master must be feeling. Gently tapping him on the arm, she hoped to get his attention before he attempted to copy his brother's maneuver.

"Mr. Marlow?"

"Yes?" he softly replied with a distant look in his eyes. "What is it, Dear?"

"May I go outside and look at the garden for a moment?"

"Yes."

As soon as the word left his lips, Alvera eagerly sprang from the couch and slipped through the glass doors, leaving him alone with Michael. Master Marlow wished that she would have stayed, but at the same time, he did not blame her for leaving. After all, he too desired to escape with her into the peace and solitude of the garden, but civility restrained him. As a guest, and an uninvited one at that, he would not repay his family's generous hospitality by making such a rude exit as his elder brother had done.

This was his struggle, and he could not confront it if he backed away in defeat. He would endure the awkward companionship of his brother no matter how excruciatingly painful the situation was for him until his mother came to the rescue. However, he would only endure it; he had no intention or desire to engage in a one-on-one conversation. But Michael seemed determined to do just the opposite.

Every time the master stole a glance at his brother, his curiosity was met with a flickering smile or twitching lips that couldn't seem to decide what they wanted to say or if they even wanted to say it at all. Before Michael could work up the courage to speak, Master Marlow rose from the couch.

Bowing slightly, he mumbled, "Excuse me," and slowly walked behind his brother. He kept his eyes on the ground and watched the aimless progression of his feet as they alternately rose and sunk into the carpet until something on the wall caught his attention. Folding his hands behind his back, he approached the wall and observed a sundry collection of portraits. He suddenly felt as if he were back in his own house standing in the forbidden room. For the past twenty years, he had forced himself to go in there every day and stare at the all-too-familiar faces that he had hung on one of the walls. They had always served as a reminder of why he could never go back. Why he was unwelcome. But now as he stood there confronting his relatives once again, their expressions did not seem as harsh and unkind as they had once appeared to him. He could look on them for the first time in a long time and actually remember happy memories. One picture, in particular, sent him back to one of the most pleasant hours of his childhood.

He was sitting between his brothers in the grass. Michael looked to be about three years old. He was dressed in a tiny pair of sky-blue suspenders with a white undershirt, and white sneakers and stockings covered his pudgy feet. His blonde curls stuck out in all different directions. It must have been humid that day. Andrew was about six years old, and he was decked out in a pair of khaki pants and a bright red short-sleeved shirt with a button-up collar. A four-year-old version of Master Marlow sat there dressed in navy shorts and a dark blue T-shirt that appeared to be a couple of sizes too large. Not one scar blemished his skinny legs, arms, or face, for this photo had been taken before he had been marred by the wolf. When he still felt fairly normal.

All three of them were smiling. Well, Michael was giggling, but it meant the same thing. The master remembered what a wonderful day that had been. It was one of the rare instances that his brothers had acted like his friends. They had gone on a picnic in a nearby park. Instead of mocking him or chasing him away, Andrew had invited the master to play with him and Michael. He remembered running through the grass in an exhilarating game of tag. He remembered climbing a massive oak tree and pretending to be a pirate looking for treasure as he perched on the gnarled branches. He remembered rolling down hills to see who could get to the bottom first. Their boyish laughter had rung through the air like a merry chorus of bells. He had been so happy, so carefree. If only he could feel that way with his family again. If only he could trust them.

Suddenly, another presence disrupted his reverie. Looking out the corner of his eye, the master saw Michael quietly standing next to him. A serene smile glowed on his face. He was admiring the same picture the master had been examining. A wistful sigh broke the tranquility of his countenance.

"This has always been my favorite picture of the three of us. It's one of the few where we all look happy together."

Master Marlow said nothing even though he could tell that Michael was waiting for a response. He was hoping to start a conversation, but the master was in no mood to talk.

In fact, he was slightly irritated with his brother for interrupting his solitude. Without giving him another sideways glance, the master turned and began walking away.

"Wait, Malchus. Please…don't keep walking away from me."

The master abruptly stopped. There was something in his brother's tone that surprised him. Intrigued, he slowly turned back around. What he saw shocked him even more. Michael's face, which had been peaceful and content only a moment before, was now utterly distorted with distress. Lines of the most agonizing grief encompassed his trembling lips. The ruddy hue that brought a youthful fullness to his bony cheeks had drained away, leaving him a ghostly white. Long purple bags, which the master had not noticed before, hung burdensomely beneath his eyes as if he had been tortured by many a sleepless night, and his crystal blue eyes themselves were brimming with tears. The master almost felt sympathy for him. What could be tormenting him so?

Michael took a shaky breath. "You don't know how happy I was when I saw you. I never thought I would have the opportunity…" he paused to recover himself.

The master watched in wonder. He had no idea that his brother had such a sensitive soul! His suffering was almost too painful to endure. However, he soon got himself under control as best he could.

Wringing his hands, he continued in a quavering voice, "I know words can never make up for past actions, but…I just wanted to tell you…how truly sorry I am for the way I treated you. I feel absolutely terrible about it. Not a day has gone by since you left that I have not felt the most violent remorse." He swallowed in an attempt to clear his throat of the emotions that threatened to incapacitate his voice. "I know I don't deserve it, but…all I ask…is that you accept my apology. If you don't…I fear I shall never be at rest again."

It was too much. All at once, Michael found himself incapable of looking at his brother any longer and broke down in a flood of tears.

"Please, forgive me, Malchus!" he choked out between sobs. "Please, forgive me!"

Master Marlow was speechless. In fact, the entire world seemed to be stunned into silence, for the only sound to be heard was the quiet sobbing of Michael, standing contritely before his brother. So, the master had not been the only one who had suffered all these years; Michael had as well, if not more so. But could he trust such a hasty and willing apology? After everything, could he be sure of its truthfulness, or was it another dark-hearted trick? He looked back at his brother's hunched figure. His crying had not abated in the slightest. Tears still flowed unceasingly down his cheeks in streams. Pure streams. He thought back to the urgency in his unsteady voice. If it had all been part of an unfeeling show, it would have come across as either melodramatic or robotic. No. It was all sincere. Michael was not a malevolent double-crosser. He never had been. He was still the same insecure little boy, pleading for guidance and forgiveness, that the master had always secretly known him to be.

Stepping closer, Master Marlow laid a gentle hand on his brother's trembling shoulder.

"Michael."

Michael jerked his tear-stained face up and was surprised to see his brother looking tenderly down at him.

"I forgave you a long time ago."

Michael's eyes and mouth widened simultaneously. He couldn't believe his ears. After staring at his brother a few moments longer, he suddenly burst into tears once again. However, this time they were not tears of sorrow; they were tears of joy.

"Thank you, Malchus!" he gasped. "Thank you!"

The master respectfully let him spend the rest of his overflow in silence. As soon as the last of his tears subsided, Michael wiped his eyes and smiled bashfully at his brother.

"So…do…do you think we could…start over? As brothers?"

Master Marlow thought about that prospect for a long while.

"Yes," he said with a nod and encouraging smile. "I'd like that very much."

6

Lost in thought, Alvera solemnly wandered around the garden. The day had warmed a bit since the beginning of their journey, and a cool autumn breeze had finally tumbled out of bed to play. It swirled in and around her powdery cloak, causing it to billow and ruffle in waves. It tugged at the ends of her hair, sending the golden strands twirling and slithering through the air like flying serpents, and it dove under every frond and petal, shaking the petrified plants to life. However, none of the wind's antics or exhilarating chills could fill Alvera with any pleasure. Her mind was preoccupied with Master Marlow.

Nothing had gone right. He had not been able to talk to his mother about the things that had been bothering him for so long, and now, he also had to face his brothers. She was worried about him. He had not mentally prepared himself for this. How would he handle it? Michael seemed reasonably affable, but she still wasn't quite sure what to make of Andrew. She felt extremely guilty for leaving the master alone in such an awkward situation, but if she had stayed, she believed that she would have been in the way. A hindrance. A third party that had no business being there. But…perhaps she should go back? No. It was better this way. This was Master Marlow's fight. A fight that he had known he would have to face one day. It may not have happened when he would have liked, but he was ready. She just knew it.

Feeling more at ease after confirming her confidence in the master, Alvera continued her tour of the garden with a lighter step. A cluster of marigolds suddenly caught her attention, and she squatted down to get a closer look. She had never seen marigolds like these before. They looked as if they had been dipped in blood. Every petal glistened with the deepest of crimson, and a fine topaz embroidery trimmed their edges. As she continued to admire the dazzling flowers, she forgot her surroundings and any possibility of being discovered.

"Didn't anyone ever tell you that it's rude to go snooping around other people's houses?"

Alvera nearly fell face-first into the flowers as she frantically scrambled to her feet. The striking figure of Andrew met her frightened eyes. He was a tall man. Not quite as tall as Master Marlow, but still a good height. Short dark umber hair speckled with a few sprigs of gray was combed neatly back on top of his head. Thick eyebrows sat sternly above his chestnut eyes, and a neatly trimmed mustache rested beneath his nose. A few lines creased his face. He wore a maroon button-up shirt that was carefully tucked into his brown pants, and a black leather belt complemented his polished dress shoes. Overall, his appearance commanded respect and dignity, but it was also tinged with a forbidding seriousness. Slightly unnerved, Alvera quickly attempted to clear herself of trespassing.

"Oh! I…I'm not snooping. Mr. Marlow gave me permission to come out here. I…I just wanted to see the garden."

Andrew suddenly burst into laughter. This was not the response she had expected, and it startled her even more than his abrupt appearance had.

"I was only teasing you!" he said with a wave of his hand. "Really, my girl. You mustn't take things so seriously."

Alvera tried to smile at the joke, but she couldn't find anything funny in it. While Andrew's amusement subsided, she turned self-consciously back toward the flowers. Perhaps if she appeared to ignore him, he would leave her alone. However, Andrew was more persistent than she had imagined. He seemed determined to talk to her, for out of the corner of her eye, she saw him slowly sauntering toward her from around the bushes he had been hiding behind.

"Alvera. Wasn't it?" he asked.

She nodded.

"How old are you, Alvera?"

"Fourteen."

"Fourteen," he repeated thoughtfully. "And…how did you and my brother— 'Mr. Marlow' I believe you call him—meet again?"

"It's exactly as he said," she replied, fiddling with an elephant ear. "I had been injured in a plane crash, and Mr. Marlow found me in the woods, took me in, and helped me."

"Ah. I see." He paused. "Where were you injured, if you don't mind my asking?"

"On my left arm. Some broken glass from one of the windows cut it from the bend of my elbow all the way up the rest of my arm when I jumped out."

"May I see it?"

Alvera instinctively looked down at her left arm. "Oh. Well…I guess…"

Before she could finish, Andrew seized her arm and began meticulously scanning its magenta scar. After a few minutes, he shook his head and released his grip. Alvera instantly drew back and held her arm protectively to her side.

"It's just as I feared," he murmured still shaking his head. "My brother's curse has spread to you."

Curse? Alvera remembered that Master Marlow had always referred to himself as cursed, but she had proved that that had been nothing more than a lie. Now, she saw where that mentality had originated…from his family. Because of his deformities, they viewed him as if he were plagued with some contagious disease, and Andrew had been poisoned by their deceitful ideology. The drawbridge to Alvera's mind instantly rose in defense. His words could not be trusted. However, she was curious as to how seriously he had been infected by such a warped view of the world, so she warily encouraged him to explain.

"What do you mean?"

"Well, my dear…I hate to tell you this, but…I'm afraid my brother has not been trying to help you at all. In fact, he's only been hurting you."

Alvera eyed him incredulously and attempted to defend the master. "No. No. You're mistaken. He …"

"Did he ever talk to you about his family?" Andrew interrupted while beginning to stalk around her.

"Yes, but …"

"What did he tell you?"

She hesitated. "Well … he said that his family didn't like him. They were ashamed of him. His brothers mocked and bullied him, and he was often alone."

"I suspected as much," he smugly acknowledged. "He's been lying to you from the start. Typical Malchus. Always wanting people to pity him for his unfortunate, deplorable condition. We were never mean or cruel to him. And if he was ever alone, it's only because he chose to be. He didn't want to be around us. In fact, he wanted nothing to do with any of his family. As you probably already know, he left as soon as he graduated high school. It was a selfish decision. He thought nothing of what it did to his poor mother. Then again, he's only ever cared about himself, even after entering the medical field. In fact, I believe the main reason he decided to become a doctor is to exact revenge.

"Ever since he was attacked by that wolf, he's been bitter. Bitter with the whole world. He believes that the world is against him. That it is completely unjust and cruel. He wants everyone to suffer as he has suffered. To feel the pain and rejection he has felt." He paused, ceased pacing, and smiled slyly at the fearful girl. "Even you, Alvera."

Stepping closer, he shrewdly examined her.

"And from the looks of things, you've come here not a moment too soon. The damage has already penetrated much deeper than your scar." He grabbed the edge of her cloak and rubbed it between his fingers. "I'm assuming *he* made this?"

"Yes," she timidly answered.

He gave a disgusted sigh and let the ethereal fabric drop back around her. "You wouldn't last a day in the real world. And judging by that vampire costume my brother wears, he wouldn't either. He wants you to be just as unable to cope with reality as he is. To dwell in a world of fantasy forever. But life is more than capes and fairy tales. There comes a time when you must put all those things behind you and grow up, or you will never succeed or even survive in this life."

He paused and stepped back. Clenching her cloak tightly around her shoulders, Alvera cautiously looked up at him. His menacing demeanor had softened. Gentle eyes gazed kindly upon her, and every other facial feature radiated with encouragement. It was a suspicious alteration.

He continued in silky tones, "Fortunately, I am willing to help you. I can teach you everything a respectable young girl, like yourself, needs to know. I can prepare you for life. All you have to do is walk away from Mr. Marlow." He extended his hand. "Let me help you, Alvera. Don't let this monster hurt you anymore."

That was it. Alvera could tolerate the lies, the biting remarks, the manipulation...but she would not allow such a scathing title to be attributed to Master Marlow. Not again. She hesitated to respond lest her immediate flare of rage should overpower her words. A deep breath of the crisp autumn air helped to quench the burning flames.

Looking as steadily and calmly as she could at him, Alvera sweetly began, "Thank you, Mr. Andrew … but … I'm afraid I must decline your offer."

Andrew's reassuring smile faded, and his outstretched hand slowly fell back to his side.

"Mr. Marlow has already offered to teach me about his practice, and I've already learned so much from him. He only has my best interests in mind and would never do anything to hurt me. I trust him."

Turning away, she slowly glided toward the house. Suddenly as if remembering something, she stopped just in front of the sliding doors and glared back at Andrew.

Defiance was firmly set in her eyes, clenched jaw, and voice as she deliberately added, "And he is *not* a monster."

As soon as the last word left her mouth, she bolted inside, fearful of the repercussions of her bold actions. Master Marlow and Michael were still standing and chatting in the den when she came scampering across the room and hid behind the master. Grabbing a section of his cloak like a security blanket, she pulled it close to her and peered around him as a frightened toddler would peer around its mother. Master Marlow flinched in alarm and confusion and looked down at her huddled figure.

"Alvera, what's the matter?"

He followed her fearful eyes over to the sliding doors just in time to see Andrew crossing the threshold. After the soft click of the door, the two of them stiffened and froze. The master met Andrew's hostile glare with his own penetrating stare. Meanwhile, Alvera glanced nervously from one opponent to the other. If they had had guns, she felt sure that they would have dueled. Suddenly, the swinging of a door shattered the intense silence that had stifled the room. Mrs. Marlow had just come back from the kitchen and was struggling to balance a platter of biscuits in one hand and a tray loaded with a steaming tea kettle and cups in the other.

"Oh! Alvera dear," she said upon spotting her. "Would you help me with the tea?"

Eager to escape the tense predicament she had found herself in, Alvera nearly sprinted to the elderly lady's side.

* * *

After partaking of the tea and biscuits, the company surprisingly settled back into genial conversation. The tension that had frozen the room with its icy fingers just moments before had now thawed and left nothing but warmth and friendliness in its wake. It was as if no altercations had ever taken place. Even Andrew seemed to be affected by the sudden change. He didn't even utter one sarcastic remark or cast any caustic glares in the master's direction! However, Alvera still warily monitored his every word and movement.

Several hours filled with laughter, illuminating stories, and fond memories passed before Master Marlow realized how late it had grown. Not wanting to abuse his family's ample generosity, he politely rose from the couch and thanked them for the wonderful visit. The others expressed how much they had enjoyed their time together as well.

"I just wish you boys could've spent more time with

each other without an old lady like me getting in the way," lamented Mrs. Marlow after giving the master a parting hug.

"Hey! That's an excellent idea!" chimed Michael. "The three of us should do something together."

"It could be like a men's night out," added Andrew.

Master Marlow thought about this grand idea in a sort of whimsical daydream. It would be wonderful to get know his brothers again. To grow closer to them. To have the brotherly bond he never thought was possible. Michael had already expressed his desire for that relationship, and who knew? Perhaps deep down inside, Andrew desired it too.

He became caught up in the boyish excitement of it all, and before he realized what he was saying, he blurted out, "Why don't we schedule an evening at my house? We could have dinner, and I could show you around."

Everyone except Alvera erupted in gleeful agreement. She couldn't believe her ears. It wasn't like the master to make such an impulsive decision. Had he suddenly become ill? She wasn't worried about Michael. He was a kind and gentle man. It was Andrew she didn't trust. In an attempt to dispel her qualms and appear as elated as the rest of the group, she forced her lips to smile. She just hoped that everything would turn out all right.

7

"Please, Sir," Felix begged while setting the table. "You're making me dizzy."

Master Marlow was pacing feverishly across the kitchen floor. Every one of his cells vibrated with nervous energy. The night of the dinner had finally arrived. Both the master and Felix had spent all day preparing the house for their guests, and now, everything was ready. All the wooden floors had been mopped and waxed until they shone with a golden amber glow. The carpet and rugs had been thoroughly vacuumed. Every possible surface that could collect dust had been wiped, and scented candles burned in every room, their therapeutic aromas mixing with the savory scents of fresh yeast rolls, boiling potatoes, and roasted chicken and vegetables now pouring from the kitchen. These tantalizing fragrances should have distracted and eased the master's troubled mind, but instead, they only caused his stomach to turn somersaults within his abdomen.

He caught the edge of the table to keep himself from wearing a rut in the floor and leaned against its smooth surface to steady the nausea slowly creeping up his throat. He swallowed it back down. "I'm sorry, Felix," he said, staring at the white tablecloth pinned beneath his quivering palms and fingers. "I'm just a little nervous. That's all."

"Nervous?" the butler replied, placing the last napkin on the table. "Don't be absurd. You're just having dinner with your brothers."

"Yes, but I haven't been around them in over twenty years. I know almost nothing of who they are now. All we have are memories." He looked up at Felix. "I want to make a good impression."

"You will, Sir. From what you told me about your first meeting at your mother's, it seems as if the three of you have already hit it off, and Andrew and Michael sound like two wonderful chaps. I'm excited to meet them." He turned toward the stove to check on the potatoes, which were beginning to froth. "Don't worry," he continued while stirring the bubbling pot. "Everything's going to be fine. Just enjoy getting to know your brothers again."

Master Marlow thought about what Felix had said. His simple yet profound words seemed to fill him with a courage that calmed his anxious heart and strengthened his trembling muscles. "You're right, Felix," he said, straightening to his full height. "You're right. Thank you."

"You're welcome, Sir."

A movement outside the kitchen window suddenly caught the butler's attention. Two pairs of headlights were bobbing up the driveway. He nearly dropped the spoon he had been using in his excitement. "Well, speaking of your brothers, Sir, they're here!"

The master's brief infusion of confidence instantly drained away along with his color. His brothers? Here? Already? His heart was beating so rapidly and with such great force that it felt and sounded like it was exploding repeatedly inside his chest. *I'm not ready*, he thought frantically to himself. *I can't do this. If I'm quick enough, maybe I can turn off all the lights and make it seem like nobody's home. No, it's too late for that. Maybe I should just hide. After all, it's just one evening. Felix can handle it himself. There'll be plenty of other opportunities.* Three sharp raps on the front door rattled his chaotic thoughts back into order. *No. I invited my brothers here to spend time with* me. *They* want *to see me, and I can't disappoint them. I can do this. I have to do this.*

Taking a deep breath and mustering as much courage as he could, Master Marlow forced himself to answer the door. He was greeted with the smiling faces of his brothers. After welcoming them to his home, the master introduced them to his butler. As soon as he heard the word "butler," Andrew immediately approached Felix. "Ah. Here," he said, thrusting his coat into Felix's surprised arms. "Be a good lad and hang this up for me, will you?"

Felix attempted to smile and did as he was told. Meanwhile, Master Marlow began giving a tour of the house. He explained that he and Felix had been doing a lot to fix it up lately. Both of them loved the colors the master had picked out for the walls, and Andrew was absolutely fascinated with the operation room. In fact, he lingered a little while longer in there while Master Marlow and Michael went into the library. Michael adored all the antique books and furniture, for he was a bit of an old soul, just like his brother.

As they continued the tour upstairs, Andrew noticed that there was one room his brother was intentionally skipping over. He jiggled the handle; it was locked.

"Say, Malchus," he called. "What's this room?"

Master Marlow turned to see which room his brother was indicating. He cringed. It was the forbidden room. The room he had turned into a study for Alvera. The room that still held so many painful memories and secrets. But he couldn't say that, especially not in front of Andrew. Quickly, he thought of a vague way to describe it. "Oh, that's just another study."

"May we see it?"

His heart skipped a beat as a pang of fear shot through his body. No! Nobody could go in there. Not with those portraits still hanging up. True, he had shared those things with Alvera and recently (though, with great reluctance) with Felix, but he trusted both of them. As of right now, such sensitive information was off limits to his brothers. "Oh! no," he said, trying not to sound too panicked. "You don't want to go in there. I…I haven't had a chance to clean it yet. It's a frightful mess. Maybe some other time?"

Andrew wasn't convinced that his brother was telling the truth, but he consented and suppressed his curiosity for the time being. After that, the master hastily finished the rest of the tour and led his guests back downstairs, where Felix announced that dinner was ready. Gathering around the table, they blessed the meal and sat down to eat.

The air was soon filled with pleasant conversations, jokes, laughter, and a warmth that emanated not only from the steaming plates of food and silver candelabra glowing in the middle of the table, but also from the hearts of everyone present. When he wasn't eating or talking, Master Marlow would look around at his merry company and smile. If this was a dream, he never wanted it to end. He was finally getting to do something that he had never thought was possible, and everyone was having a grand time. Everything was perfect.

By the end of the meal, everyone had fallen into sharing hilarious things that had recently happened to them. As Michael finished his tale, Andrew prepared to give his.

"If you think that was something, you're not going to believe what happened to me at work the other day." He paused to take a swig of his water, and Michael did the same. Felix took the opportunity to clear away some of the dishes. While everyone was thus occupied, Andrew leaned over toward his brother and whispered, "Oh, Malchus, you've got a little…" he discreetly indicated the rest of the thought by tapping his nose.

Embarrassed, Master Marlow snatched up his napkin and thoroughly wiped the underside of his nose while Andrew continued his story. A burning sensation suddenly overpowered all his senses. It felt as if a wildfire had suddenly roared to life and was now racing up and down his sinuses. The flames were so intense that they caused his eyes to water. He closed his eyelids tightly against the sweltering heat and pressed a hand into his throbbing forehead, hoping the stinging would soon subside. Michael noticed his brother's pained expression and leaned closer to check on him.

"Malchus, are you all right?"

Master Marlow looked up and was surprised to see Michael's innocent blue eyes concernedly scanning his face. Despite the angry fire still raging inside his head, he managed to flash a reassuring smile. "Yes, I'm fi…" The rest of the word was sucked away by a sharp breath as the acrid burning was replaced with a violent irritation that resulted in an explosive sneeze.

"Oh! bless you, Malchus!" Michael said.

"Bless you, Sir!" Felix said simultaneously.

He sneezed again.

This time, they responded in rapid succession.

"Bless you!"

"Oh, dear."

Feeling yet another sneeze coming, Master Marlow abruptly rose from the table, excused himself, and made his way to the library. Felix stood up as well.

"I'll go get a handkerchief."

"No need, my good man," Andrew suddenly cried, stopping the butler before he could even take two steps toward the stairs. "I've got one." Without another word, he hurried down the hall to the library. He found his brother standing in the middle of the room with his head buried in the bend of his elbow.

"Here you go, Malchus."

The master tentatively raised his head to look at his brother, but when he spotted the handkerchief in his outstretched hand, he retracted and waved him away.

"No, no, really. I…AAACHOO!!!"

Andrew stepped closer and urged the master with a firm yet gentle voice. "You need it."

Master Marlow turned and looked from the handkerchief to his brother. He didn't want to take it, but when he felt another sneeze welling up, he finally consented and grabbed the cloth offering. After his fit subsided and he finished blowing his nose, the two brothers walked back to the table together. Master Marlow sat back down, but he couldn't force himself to meet anyone else's gaze. Instead, he resorted to staring down at his lap.

"I'm terribly sorry, everyone," he solemnly began while fiddling with his handkerchief. "Please, forgive me. I've never had anything like this happen before."

Sympathetic condolences erupted all around the table. Michael reached out and laid a hand on his brother's arm.

"No, it's all right, Malchus. These things happen." He chuckled. "Why, I remember one time I had such a fit that lasted nearly fifteen minutes! I never thought I was going to stop sneezing!"

"Yes, Michael's right," agreed Andrew. "Besides, I'm sure people everywhere make utter fools of themselves in front of their brothers, whom they haven't seen in over twenty years, every day."

As if he had just sat on a tack, Felix jumped out of his chair, nearly knocking it off its feet in the process. Any remaining thoughts concerning Andrew's snide remark were instantly stunned into silence. All eyes were glued to the butler's, which were glowing like fiery red coals. Master

Marlow stared in shock and wonder. He had never seen Felix so angry before. In fact, he didn't even know that Felix was capable of being angry, for he had always been so mild and patient in almost every situation. Now, he looked like an enraged goat ready to maul someone with his horns. It was a truly frightening transformation.

"That's it!" he bellowed in an unearthly voice. (The master had to do a double take to make sure that it was really Felix who had spoken.) "I have tolerated your rudeness until I can't stand it anymore. You will *not* insult Master Marlow like that and get away with it." He pointed toward the front door and confronted Andrew with the most intense glare he could muster. "Leave this house at once."

Andrew stared seemingly dumbfounded at the irate butler as if he failed to understand what he had done wrong. His gaping mouth twitched as if he were trying to find the right words to defend his position, but before he could stutter one syllable, Master Marlow held up a mediating hand. "Felix," he softly spoke in a weary voice, "it's all right." Slowly, as if with great difficulty, he rose from his chair and looked gravely around at the company before him. "Thank you all for coming. I hope you enjoyed yourselves."

"Well, I don't know about everyone else," Andrew most inappropriately chimed after springing merrily from his seat, "but, I *certainly* enjoyed myself. We should *really* do this more often." He chuckled as he went to retrieve his coat from the closet under the stairs. All the while, Felix's searing glare did not abate. The master fancied that he even saw lasers shooting from his eyes and scorching the back of his brother's head. As Andrew finished buttoning up his coat, Master Marlow opened the front door for him.

"Thank you, Malchus. Well, have a gesundheit…I mean…a good night." Even after the dark swallowed his figure, Andrew's laughter still echoed eerily through the night like the wild yipping of a coyote.

Meanwhile, Michael stood like a zombie in the background. He had already slipped on his own coat, but he found himself unable to follow his brother out the door. All he could do was helplessly watch those terrible events unfold and replay over and over again against the cold, rectangular void gaping before him. His eyes involuntarily wandered over to his brother, and as soon as he saw his face, he was awakened from his hazy stupor.

The master's head hung low as if it were being weighed down by a pile of books. His eyes were only opened to about the size of a crescent, but it was enough to allow his brother to see his glazed pupils staring through the floor. Tired bags sighed beneath his eyes. Overall, he would have had a rather ghostly appearance if it weren't for the unnatural rosy hue burning against his cheeks and nose. Perhaps it was a leftover flush from sneezing so much, a reaction against the frigid wind now chafing his skin, a blush of embarrassment, or some combination of the three. Michael couldn't decide, but it didn't matter.

Finally detaching his feet from the floor, he made his way over to his brother. He gave him that same earnest look he had given him at the table and waited for him to return it before he spoke.

"I'm sorry, Malchus," he said in a voice that was barely

above a whisper. To Michael's surprise, he thought he saw the flicker of a smile illuminate his brother's face. It was followed by a shake of his head.

"You don't have anything to apologize for."

His words ripped apart the fragile seams of Michael's heart. His brother was so strong. So kind. He never blamed anyone for anything even after everything he had been through. Even after tonight. Michael suddenly turned away as tears sprang to his eyes. He managed to hold them in and looked back at his brother.

"Are you sure you're all right?"

The master hesitated before taking a deep breath and answering, "I will be." The two looked at each other one last time before the master broke the silence once more. "Well, thank you again for coming, Michael. Drive safe."

"I will. Good night, Malchus."

"Good night."

Master Marlow watched Michael get into his car before shutting the door and slouching against its hard surface. As soon as Felix heard the click of the latch, he broke into a violent rant.

"I've never met a more malevolent person in my entire life! I can't believe I was excited to meet *him*! Of all the nerve! 'Be a good lad and hang this up for me, will you?'! No 'sir' or 'thank you!' What does he think I am?! A slave?! But that was just the beginning! He couldn't say a single sentence without throwing in a sarcastic remark! And the way he spoke to *you*! After *you* invited *him* here! The ungrateful scoundrel! Well, he better not expect any more warm welcomes from me unless it's in the form of a few choice words! In fact, the next time I see him, I'm going to ..."

And the list went on and on, but the master didn't hear any of it. His mind was too preoccupied with the events of the night. The evening had been a disaster. And it had started off so well! *I had such high hopes for tonight*, he thought dismally, *but I always ruin everything. Perhaps I'm never meant to have a good relationship with my family.* It was all too much to handle between Andrew's bullying and his own self-loathing. He wanted to cry, but instead, he found himself laughing. Laughing! He had been overtaken by a complete state of hysteria, and he had no idea why. For a moment, he wondered if he had gone mad. No. That couldn't be right. He wouldn't have enough sense to even ask such a question if he were mad. Perhaps it was from absentmindedly watching Felix animatedly throwing up his arms, swaggering across the floor, and pointing fingers at imaginary adversaries while he continued to fume and rave. Whatever the reason, he couldn't stop laughing until a sneeze caught him by surprise.

Felix immediately stopped pacing and looked concernedly at the master. "Are you sure you're all right, Sir?"

"Yes! I'm quite sure," he snapped, suddenly exasperated. "I say! Someone else could sneeze and no one would think anything of it. But when *I* start sneezing, the whole world comes to a stop!"

"It's not that, Sir. It's just ...in all the time that I've known you, you've rarely ever been sick."

That last word did it. He couldn't stand it any longer. Giving Felix a sharp look, Master Marlow stalked aggressively toward the frightened butler. He stopped just a few inches in front of him and loomed menacingly over him like a vulture waiting for its next victim to keel over. His cold, igneous eyes bore down on the butler's bushy head, causing his curls to shiver in the bitter frost. After remaining in this imposing position for several minutes, the master slowly leaned closer, and in a voice that could have chilled even the hottest volcano, he said, pronouncing each word with deliberate force, "I'm not…sick."

He glared at the butler for a moment longer to make sure his message sunk in before dramatically turning around and marching up the stairs. About halfway up, he was overtaken by another sneeze. He paused and quivered with rage. He could almost feel Felix's concerned gaze penetrating his back as if to say, "I told you so." Taking a deep breath and stiffening his back in defiance, the master continued on up the stairs. Felix watched his every movement, even after he had vanished into one of the rooms in the upper hall. Resisting the urge to follow and console him, he reluctantly turned back toward the kitchen to begin cleaning up. Master Marlow needed time to himself. Things would be better in the morning. But somehow, Felix couldn't convince himself of that.

8

Over the next few days, Master Marlow's sneezes subsided, but they were replaced by a nagging cough. He thought it might just be a slight irritation in his throat from the excess mucus that had built up from his fit the other night, but it never went away. In fact, it only grew worse. However, it wasn't bad enough to keep him from work, so he continued his daily routines as normal. He hoped that by doing so, he would dispel any remaining fears Felix had concerning his health, for ever since that night, the butler had been carefully monitoring everything the master did and began checking on him more often than usual. It was getting to be rather annoying, particularly because it was getting harder and harder to fool him. But when the weekend finally arrived, the master realized that there was no way he could keep his condition a secret any longer.

It was a bright Saturday morning, one of those rare days in winter when the sun manages to melt away a patch of that snowy blanket in the sky. Its rays, pale from lack of use, tried to warm as much of the gray earth as they could before they were forced into hibernation once again. Standing in front of the kitchen window, Felix took advantage of what little heat they had to offer as well. He couldn't stand there long, however, for he had breakfast to make. Rummaging in one of the cabinets below the sink, he pulled out a pan and grabbed four eggs from the refrigerator. He was about to go upstairs and ask Master Marlow how he would like his eggs, when he heard a heavy footfall on the stairs.

"Ah, good morning, Sir," he cheerfully greeted, grabbing the pan and an egg and hurrying over to meet the master on his way down. "I was just about to come get you. How would you like your …"

The rest of his sentence ended with a splat as the egg slipped from his hand and shattered in a sticky mess on the floor. He was too stunned by what he saw descending the stairs to move or speak. Master Marlow was all but unrecognizable. His raven hair looked as if it hadn't been brushed in a week; it stuck out in wild tufts all over his head. Several dark rings sagged beneath his puffy, half-asleep eyes, and his cheeks and nose glowed with a feverish flush. Wrinkled pajamas hung haphazardly on his staggering body, and a pair of house slippers threatened to slide off his feet with every burdensome step.

"Sir!" Felix said, finally finding his voice. "You look awful!"

The master cast him a withering look. "Thang you for doticing."

"And you sound even worse!"

Ignoring that last comment, he shuffled past the shocked butler, pulled out a chair at the kitchen table, sat down, tilted his head back, and closed his eyes. Felix turned and carefully observed his pitiful figure. His chest rose and fell laboriously with every congested breath. It was painful to watch, but even more painful to listen to. His breathing sounded like wheezing gasps for air. Something was wrong. Terribly wrong.

Slowly, the butler approached the ailing doctor. "Sir," he timidly began, "I know you don't like hearing this, but ... there really is no denying it any longer. You are sick."

His only response was a series of crackling coughs.

"*Very* sick."

"I dow," the master moaned.

"Well, then," Felix said, setting the pan on the table. "Come on. Let's get you back into bed." He tried to help the master out of his chair, but he only waved him away.

"Doh, doh."

"Oh, come now, Sir. You need to rest. It's the only way you're going to get better."

Master Marlow just shook his head. He was being stubborn. The butler was going to have to try a different tactic if he were going to have any success.

"Why don't you take some medicine then?"

"I already have."

"Well, it doesn't seem to be working."

The master sighed, "It just has to rud its course. That's all."

"Well, you can let it run its course in bed. Now, come on."

"Doh," he protested, rising from his seat and shaking his head once again. "I'b fide."

Felix watched helplessly as the master lurched away from him across the floor. He wanted to retort with a "No, you're not," but instead, he simply released a defeated huff, meandered back over to the stove, and began pulling out all the necessary utensils for cooking.

"Well, at least have some breakfast."

"Doh, thang you, Feligs," he said as he approached the side door. "I'b dot hugry. I'b just goig to go outside for a little bit ad get sobe fresh air."

"Oh! really, Sir! You must eat something. You need to keep up your strength. At least have a glass of orange juice!"

The closing of a door was his only answer.

"Oh, why bother," he sighed, leaning an elbow against the counter and glaring at the unnecessary mess of dishes he had created. "They say men are bad patients, but I think doctors are even worse." Suddenly, in the midst of his sulking, he got a brilliant idea that brightened his whole countenance. "Well, since I've already got everything out, I'll make him some tea. It'll do his body good."

The master had not returned by the time Felix had finished boiling the water and steeping the tea bags in the kettle, so he decided to go ahead and pour some of the healing liquid into the cups. When he still didn't come back, the butler decided to take the tea out to him before it got too cold. Balancing the tray loaded with the kettle, cups, and saucers in one hand, he opened the side door with the other and proceeded out to the garden.

"Sir," he called as he rounded the fence, "I made you some tea. I know you said you didn't want anything, but …"

Felix jerked to a stop, losing his hold on the tray. It hit the ground with an ear-splitting crash. Glass flew in all directions, and every last drop of the precious tea that he had worked so hard to make for the master seeped into the ground. But Felix didn't notice any of that, nor did he care. He was much more concerned about something else.

"SIR!!!"

9

Alvera merrily skipped up the hill to Master Marlow's house. In one of his recent letters, he had told her that he hadn't been feeling well lately, so she thought she'd surprise him by coming over to visit. Perhaps it would help him feel a little better or at least cheer him up. But once she made it to the top, an alarming sight subdued her springy step and sent her optimism sliding off her shoulders and rolling all the way back to the bottom of the hill. In the left portion of the yard next to the garden, Felix was kneeling beside a dark, motionless figure. An icy rush of adrenaline flooded Alvera's veins, shocking her heart into a frenzied rhythm. She recognized the figure; it was Master Marlow.

Breaking into a sprint, she raced across the tan lawn toward them.

"Mr. Felix! What happened?!"

"I . . . I don't know!" he said looking confusedly back and forth between Alvera and the unconscious doctor. "I was making tea, and when I came outside to give him some, I found him collapsed on the ground! Here." He lifted the master's lolling head onto his lap. "Can you help me get him inside?"

Alvera nodded and scurried toward the master's lower half. Slipping her arms under his bent knees, she lifted his legs while Felix hoisted up his torso and supported his head and neck. In this manner, they quickly and carefully carried him into the house, up the stairs, and to his room. Once they were there, they gently lowered him onto his bed. They paused for just a moment to catch their breath, for both of them were panting quite hard by the time they released their load. It wasn't easy for a lanky butler and a skinny little girl to carry a full-grown and rather large-boned man, who was taller than both of them, all that distance (not to mention up an entire flight of stairs). Once they had recovered, they removed his slippers and pulled up the covers. Both stepped back and simply gawked, horrified by the awful sight before them.

Master Marlow lay as still as a corpse. The only signs of life were the short, shuddering breaths ruffling the blankets. Massive drops of sweat crawled like slugs across his skin, leaving dewy trails all over his flushed face and plastering whisps of hair to his forehead. A pained expression rested heavily on his scrunched brows and eyes and seemed to bind him in his unnatural sleep. Alvera's heart began to throb with the same aching pain the master must have been feeling. She had never seen him like this before, and it terrified her.

"I have no idea what's wrong with him," Felix said in a small voice. "I mean … I knew he was sick, but I didn't know he was this bad off." Slowly, he turned his head toward Alvera, an idea flickering in his owl-like eyes. "Do … do you think you could figure it out?"

Alvera slowly turned away from the sickly form on the bed and looked up at the expectant butler. His face glowed with a pallid hue in the stifling darkness of the room, and his amber eyes grew wider with every passing second as they desperately searched for even the faintest shimmer of hope. He was just as scared as she was, but unlike him, she had to mask her fear. Felix was a worrier and did not handle stress very well. She had to be strong for the both of them. She had to be his beacon of hope.

Her eyes burning with as much confidence as she could feign, Alvera said, "I can try," and began examining the doctor. Gently brushing a few strands of his drenched hair aside, she placed the back of her palm against his forehead. She gasped and instantly jerked her hand away as if it had just touched a hot stove. *He's burning up!* she thought anxiously. Next, she grabbed his wrist and checked his pulse. It was slightly elevated, but it was nothing to be too concerned about. Leaning down, she rested her ear against his chest and listened to his breathing. It wasn't clear. She was going to have to try a different method if she were going to get any positive results.

"Mr. Felix," she said steadily without looking away from her patient.

"Yes?"

"Could you bring me a stethoscope, a thermometer, a bowl of cold water, and a washcloth?"

"Yes, of course!" He dashed out of the room. With his nervous energy, he returned in less than a minute.

"Thank you," Alvera said as he placed the items on the nightstand beside the bed. She immediately stuck the thermometer in the master's mouth. While it calculated his temperature, she slipped on the stethoscope and listened to his lungs once again. A terrible rattling crackled in her ears. It sounded as if he were breathing in shards of broken glass. That could only mean one thing, but she couldn't be sure until she knew what his temperature was. Removing the stethoscope from her ears and letting it fall back around her neck, she pulled the thermometer out of the master's mouth and closely examined its reading: 40°C. *Forty degrees Celsius!* she repeated to herself in disbelief.

Her face must have revealed her shock, for from the back of the room where he was wringing his hands while standing guard like a vigilant soldier, Felix timidly asked, "What is it?"

Straightening, she said, "He has a dangerously high fever."

The butler's mouth went dry, leaving him speechless for a moment. However, he finally worked up the courage to ask the most important question of all. "So, can you tell what's wrong with him?"

She nodded. "He has a severe case of pneumonia."

"Pneumonia?" he repeated, feeling faint with terror. "Oh, dear!"

"He needs immediate medical attention."

"Should…should I call the hospital then?" he queried, inching toward the door.

"No, there's no time for that."

Felix gave her a puzzled look. Seeing his confusion, she quickly explained.

"What I mean is we need to start his treatment right now. This very minute. Here," she said, handing him the washcloth before he could panic. "I'm going to need your help. Soak this in the cold water and lay it across his forehead. When it gets warm, repeat the process. All right?"

"All right."

"Ok. I'll be right back."

With that, Alvera raced out the door, down the stairs, and into the operation room. Flinging open one of the upper cabinets, she scanned the rows and rows of bottles for the right medicine. She grabbed two bottles of pills at first, but upon further consideration, she traded one out for the same medicine in a liquid form. *It'll be easier to get liquids in him at this point*, she reasoned. There was just one more thing to get, but as Alvera prepared to open another cabinet, she suddenly froze. A startling realization chilled her fluttering heart with fear. She had forgotten what the third item was! *Oh, no!* her mind ghostly whispered. *What was it? What was it?!* A hysterical frenzy crashed over her like an icy tsunami. In a desperate attempt to remember, she darted around the room and threw open every door, cabinet, and drawer. They were filled with assortments of syringes, beakers, needles, knives, sterilizing equipment, and strange devices; but nothing sparked any recollection. Nothing!

After rummaging through every possible compartment, she finally calmed down and forced herself to stand still and think. It was some kind of machine. She knew that much. But what was it? What was it called? She began to grow frustrated and squinted her eyes shut in order to concentrate better. *I know this!* She thought back to some of her recent lessons with Master Marlow. *What did he say it was?* She had to remember. She just had to, for she was the only one who could. The master's life depended on her.

Suddenly, her eyes flew open as an alleviating light flooded her mind. *A nebulizer! That's it!* She rushed over to the cabinet beside the incubator. As soon as she opened the door, there it was, staring right at her: the nebulizer. *And the antibiotics should already be with it.* Peering at its see-through hatch, she saw the small bottle safely nestled inside.

Gathering all her needed supplies, Alvera scampered to the kitchen, filled a small glass with water, and leaped up the stairs like a nimble deer. Once she was back in the room, she relieved Felix of his duty, set the washcloth and bowl aside, and placed the rest of the items on the nightstand.

"What do we do now?" he asked.

"Well, we need to give him some of this to help reduce his fever," she said, holding up the bottle full of syrupy liquid, "but first, we're going to have to wake him up." Setting the bottle back down and kneeling next to the bed, she leaned close to the master's ear as if she were about to whisper a secret. "Mr. Marlow."

No response. She called his name again a little louder.

"Mr. Marlow."

Still no response. She tried tapping him lightly on the shoulder.

"Wake up, Mr. Marlow. Wake up."

She tapped harder.

"Please, Mr. Marlow. You have to wake up."

Nothing. Growing more anxious by the second, she tapped even harder.

"Come on, Mr. Marlow. Wake up. Please, wake up!"

Alvera suddenly held her breath. She thought she saw movement, but after several excruciatingly long seconds of staring at his stone-like face, she began to doubt her eyes. No! Wait! There it was again. Yes! She knew she had seen it. His mouth twitched. Soon, it was followed by a scrunching up of his eyes. In fact, his whole body began to squirm beneath the sheets while various grunts and moans escaped his lips. Finally, his eyelids fluttered indecisively before slowly prying themselves open. After adjusting to the dim light, his eyes scanned the room before focusing on Alvera. She smiled compassionately at their ebony orbs.

"Hello, Mr. Marlow. It's me, Alvera. I'm here to help you, ok?"

He slowly blinked and tilted his head in a slight nod as if to indicate that he understood.

Rising to her feet, she turned toward Felix and said, "We need to sit him up, so he can take the medicine. Can you help me?"

Nodding, Felix hurried over to the other side of the bed. Both put an arm under each of his and a hand on his back.

"You got him?" Alvera asked.

"Yes."

"Ok, Mr. Marlow. We're going to sit you up now, all

right?" She addressed Felix once again. "On the count of three. One … two … threeee!"

Alvera had to dig her feet into the floor and put her whole weight against the master in order to help Felix push him up. It felt like trying to move a potato sack full of rocks, for the master was too weak and delirious to help them. It was all dead weight. However, they managed to sit him up and prop some pillows behind his back.

"All right," Alvera gasped, trying to catch her breath again. "Can you keep him steady while I give him the medicine?"

"Yes."

Releasing her grip on the master, she turned toward the nightstand and measured out the right dosage of medicine in a tiny plastic cup. It was a bright red concoction with a strong scent of cherry licorice that made Alvera's stomach flop around like a flounder. She just hoped the master wouldn't object to its vile odor.

"All right, Mr. Marlow," she said, showing him the cup. "I need you to take this. It's going to help you. Can you open your mouth for me?"

He did so obediently like a baby bird patiently waiting for his mother to feed him, and she carefully raised the cup to his lips and poured its contents in. Afterwards, she grabbed the glass of water and gave him some of it to drink to help wash down any residue that the medicine might have left behind. The water must have gone down the wrong way, for immediately after swallowing it, the master began coughing and sputtering. Alarmed, Felix looked to Alvera.

"What should I do?"

"Just pat him on the back and let him get it all out," she said while connecting the hose, cup, and mouthpiece to the motor of the nebulizer.

He did just as she said, and shortly, the master's hacking came to a stop. "There you go, Sir," he soothed, switching his pats to a rub. "It's all right." He looked over at the strange machine Alvera was fiddling with. "What's that?"

"It's called a nebulizer. It's a machine that will help open up his airway and get these antibiotics to his lungs more quickly than if he took them orally."

Felix smiled. Alvera had thought of everything. He couldn't express how relieved he was that she was there. Suddenly, he felt pressure against his hand and looked down. The master was pushing against him. "Oh…uh…Alvera. Alvera!" She turned to see what was the matter. "I can't keep him up. He's trying to lie back down."

Quickly, Alvera finished pouring the antibiotics into the nebulizer's medicine cup, screwed on the mouthpiece, clipped it to the side of the machine, and came to Felix's aid. "No, Mr. Marlow," she grunted as they struggled to force him back up. "I need you to stay awake just a little bit longer."

A heart-wrenching groan rumbled in his throat as soon as he was sitting up straight again, and his hands and feet began fidgeting and kicking at the blanket. He was growing restless and agitated. They would have to work quickly before he decided to stop cooperating.

"All right," she said, bringing the mouthpiece toward

him. "I need you to open your mouth for me one more time."

He instantly jerked his head away.

"Mr. Marlow."

She tried again, and he jerked his head in the other direction.

"Come on."

For several more minutes, she chased him in this manner from one side of the bed to the other, alternately coaxing and pleading with him, but it was all in vain.

"Please, Mr. Marlow. Please take it."

Finally, he had had enough of their little game and forcefully pushed the mouthpiece away.

"Oh!" Alvera cried in despair. Feeling hot tears of frustration and shame boil up in her eyes, she hung her head as if in defeat. What was she to do? He had to take this medicine. If he didn't, she feared that…*No. Don't even think about that*, she suddenly chided herself. *You can't give up. No matter how much he fights against you, you have to keep trying.*

With a new resolve, she raised her head back up and prepared to try again, when a startling sight caused her to shudder and blush. Master Marlow was staring right at her, and somehow, he seemed even more unlike himself than he had just a few moments ago. His whole body had begun to shiver, a delayed reaction to his fever. His clammy hands clutched insecurely at the crumpled portion of blanket heaped in his lap. Her eyes travelled up to his face. Both his nose and mouth trembled. And his eyes. His eyes! They were the most pitiful things she had ever seen. They were glossy and tinged with pink.

A wild look like that of a cornered animal contracted their pupils, and their deep pits quivered as they anxiously scanned the girl's fearful face that had suddenly become unfamiliar to them. She could almost hear their intense gaze whimpering, "Why are you doing this to me?" One of the tears that she had been trying so hard to fight back suddenly spilled over as she noticed several drops of dew sparkling in the corners of the master's own eyes. She understood. He was disoriented. He didn't know where he was or who anyone was around him, and it frightened him.

Without breaking the delicate connection between crystal and onyx eyes, Alvera tentatively reached out and cradled one of the master's burning cheeks in her small hand. The initial contact startled him, but after a few seconds, he visibly calmed under her gentle touch.

"Listen, Mr. Marlow," she tenderly whispered. "I know you're scared and don't feel well…but I'm here to help you. You can trust me. Now, I need you to take this. It will make you feel so much better. All right? Please, Mr. Marlow. This is the last thing I need you to do. And after that, you can sleep 'till your heart's content. I promise. Just do this one last thing for me, and then we're done. Please."

Felix froze and held his breath. In fact, the entire room seemed to do the same in anxious anticipation of what would happen next. All eyes watched in silent awe as Alvera and Master Marlow simply continued to stare into each other's souls. Slowly blinking his eyes, the master broke the spell and opened his mouth. Alvera's eyes grew wide. It was the loudest "yes" she could have ever heard. A huge smile glowed on her face.

"Thank you, Mr. Marlow! Thank you!" She gave him the mouthpiece, lifted the hatch of the machine, and placed her finger over the switch. "Ok. As soon as I press this button, I need you to breathe in through your mouth and out through your nose. All right?"

He nodded, and she turned it on, the motor humming to life.

"All right. Breathe in through your mouth and out through your nose. In through your mouth and out through your nose."

The master followed her directions perfectly, and soon, they were in rhythm together.

"Good. Keep going. I'll tell you when to stop."

After about fifteen minutes, the medicine cup was empty, and Alvera turned the machine off.

"Good job!" she said, patting the master on the back and removing the mouthpiece. "That's it. You're all done." As soon as he heard those words, he let his eyelids droop, plopped back on his pillows, and instantly fell asleep. Alvera grinned sympathetically. *Poor thing! He must be exhausted.* After adjusting his pillows and pulling the blanket back up around his chin, she stepped back, closed her eyes, and sighed. Felix watched her for a moment before timidly inching forward.

"Is ... is he going to be all right?"

Alvera slowly opened her eyes, looked from Felix back to Master Marlow, and sighed again. "I hope so."

10

Alvera refused to leave Master Marlow. For hours, she sat by his sleeping side and tirelessly monitored his condition. Sometimes, she would reapply the cool washcloth across his forehead. Other times, she would simply talk to him, and on a few occasions, Felix thought he heard her softly humming some sweet melody. Dear Alvera! What a kind and generous spirit! She could have been doing sundry fun activities for her own pleasure like so many other children, but instead, she chose to spend her weekend caring for the one she loved. Knowing that he was sick, there was nowhere else she would rather be and nothing else she would rather be doing. These precious thoughts lightened the butler's heavy mind and heart as he went about his own chores, for he knew that the master was in good hands.

Soon, evening crept upon the little wooden house and flashed her fleeting goldenrod, peach, and magenta smile through the windows at its inhabitants. It was a subtle reminder to Felix that it was growing late. Softly pattering up to the master's room and finding Alvera still faithfully sitting in her chair next to his bed, he gently urged her to go on home and get some rest. She insisted that she wasn't tired, but Felix could tell by her eyes that she was. Besides, he wanted to make sure she made it home before it got dark.

Reluctantly, she consented, but before she left, she showed Felix how to use the nebulizer and gave him detailed instructions concerning everything else. He was to administer the antibiotics with the nebulizer twice a day, and he needed to continue giving the master the liquid medication until his fever was completely gone. The other medicine was to help alleviate coughing, but he didn't need to give that to the master until he had improved considerably. Right now, he needed to get as much phlegm and fluid out of his lungs as possible, and the only way to do that was by forcefully coughing it up. It wouldn't be pleasant, but it was something that had to be done. Lastly, he needed to make sure that the master drank plenty of fluids.

Once she was sure that Felix understood, Alvera turned back to Master Marlow, told him goodbye and that she hoped he would get better soon, leaned over, and tenderly kissed him on the forehead. She also gave Felix a parting hug. He assured her that he would take good care of the master. She had no doubts about that. After pausing in the doorway and waving, she made her way down the stairs and finally headed home.

***

The first thing he was aware of was the darkness. It encased him like a cozy, cotton cocoon. He didn't want to leave its comforting embrace, but at the same time, its blanketing arms had wrapped themselves so tightly about him that he felt that they were beginning to suffocate him. He had to break free. Slowly, he forced his way out of their strangling hold, and the darkness rolled away like a window shade being lifted up to let in the first energizing rays of dawn. A blurred light pricked his eyes, and he instantly closed them again, regretting his decision. However, after blinking a few more times, his eyes adjusted to the brightness (really just the dim glow of a lamp), and the room came into focus. He stared straight ahead at a spruce wall, trying to piece things together. His aching head throbbed with the effort. He couldn't remember anything that had happened, and nothing seemed familiar.

Suddenly, he became conscious of a great pressure on his chest. He looked down, but nothing was there. It felt as if a great steel safe were smothering his lungs. Taking a deep breath, he tried to lift its weight, but in the process, his breath hitched in his throat, sending him into a violent coughing fit.

Felix, who had fallen asleep in a chair in a corner of the room, jolted at the sound. His arms and legs flailed wildly as he tried to scramble into a more alert position. "I'm up! I'm up!"

Once his fit subsided, Master Marlow followed the source of the voice with his eyes and finally noticed Felix sitting at the foot of the bed. He squinted at his shadowy figure. "Feligs?"

The butler's eyes grew as wide as his gaping mouth. He couldn't believe it. Was he dreaming? No. This was real. His eyes began to water, and an overjoyed smile trembled on his lips as an overwhelming relief flooded his insides.

"Oh, Sir! You're awake! You're finally awake!" He bounced out of his chair to the master's side and threw his arms around his neck. "Oh, thank goodness! I was so worried about you! Oh!" he cried, abruptly pulling away and looking over at the clock. "What time is it?" The hands indicated that it was just after 6:00 A.M. "Well, it's a bit early, but I'll go ahead and give you your next treatment. It certainly won't hurt."

Making his way to the other side of the bed, Felix grabbed the thermometer off the nightstand. "Let's see how your temperature is." He stuck it in the master's mouth and waited. After a few seconds, it beeped to signal it was done, and he eagerly examined its reading. It had dropped considerably from yesterday. That meant that the medicine was working.

"Oh, much better! However, you still have a slight fever, so I'll go ahead and give you another dose of medicine."

Meanwhile, Master Marlow absentmindedly stared at the ceiling. He didn't seem to be paying much attention to what Felix was saying or doing, for he was still trying to recollect even the smallest sliver of information that might explain the strange situation he found himself in. However, no matter how long he stared at that monotonously blank sheet, he couldn't get anything to surface. He finally resorted to voicing his questions.

"Where ab I?"

The butler paused in his work and looked over at the

master. His cheerful countenance fell. "Why, at home, Sir. In your room."

The doctor groggily scanned the dark space and slowly began to recognize it. Yes, this was his room.

"How log have I bed here?"

"Since yesterday morning."

"What day is it today?"

"Sunday, Sir."

"Suday?" he said, his weary eyes opening a little wider. "I deed to get ready for church." Even as weak as he was, the master managed to wriggle halfway out of bed, and he probably would have succeeded in getting all the way out if Felix hadn't been there to stop him.

"Oh, no, Sir!" he said, forcing him to lie back down and covering him back up with his blanket. "I'm afraid you can't go to church today. You're very, very sick. You need to stay in bed and rest."

"But…" The rest of the master's protest was drowned out by a sneeze that sounded more like a snort because he was so congested.

"Bless you." Felix opened the top drawer of the nightstand, pulled out a clean handkerchief, and gave it to the master. After he finished blowing his nose, the butler gave him the medicine for his fever.

Master Marlow stared back up at the ceiling and grimaced, but he wasn't sure if he did so because of the awful taste the medicine left in his mouth or because of the dull pain pulsating throughout his body. His head felt as if it had swelled to three times its size, and its throbbing pounded in his ears. An intense pressure pushed against the backs of his eyes, causing them to flinch even at the faintest ember of light. It felt as if ten handkerchiefs had been stuffed up his nose and kept expanding. His throat felt as if it had been shredded by a feral cat, and his chest ached every time he took a breath. He had never felt so awful in his entire life. What was the matter? He gingerly rolled his head toward Felix.

"What's wrog with be?"

The butler looked over and met his pitiful gaze. "You have pneumonia, Sir."

"Deubodia?" he repeated, wrinkling his forehead. "But…that doesd't bake ady seds. Bost cases of deubodia ared't codtagious, ad I haved't bed aroud ady patiedts with…" He couldn't finish his puzzling thoughts, for he was overpowered by another series of lung-rattling coughs.

"Easy, Sir! Easy!" Felix soothed while alternately patting and rubbing his back. "Don't worry about that right now. Just rest."

As the last of his coughs faded, the master gave a frustrated sigh and sank back into his pillow. He felt so helpless. Suddenly, a movement to his right distracted him from his irritation. Felix was busily preparing the nebulizer.

"I did't dow you dew how to use a debulizer," he commented, rather impressed.

"I didn't," the butler corrected with a smile. "Alvera showed me how."

"Alvera?" he said, his brow creasing with confusion once again. "She was here?"

Felix turned away from his work and looked at the master with even more concern than he had before. "Yes, Sir. Don't…don't you remember?"

Master Marlow plunged into the innermost recesses of his mind. All his memories from the day before were shrouded in a dense fog. He knew they were there, but he just couldn't grasp them. However, the more he groped about within the obscuring haze, the more it began to dissipate, until it finally dissolved altogether. He could see it all clearly now. There he was, walking out to the garden. He remembered feeling unsteady as if he were stumbling through a cloud. Suddenly, everything had begun to spin and blur together until it was nothing but darkness. But then the darkness broke, and…yes, there it was. Her face emerged and solidified out of the rippling waters. Alvera's loving face, looking tenderly upon him. She had been there diligently taking care of him in his most dire hour. He closed his eyes, taking comfort in the recollection of her soothing presence.

"Yes. Dow I rebeber." After a moment of reposing in this peaceful manner, his eyes reopened as another thought occurred to him. "Where is she dow?"

"Oh, I sent her home yesterday evening, Sir. Otherwise, she'd still be here." A glowing smile tugged at his stubby beard and almost seemed to make it grin. "What a dear, sweet child! She never once left your side."

The nebulizer was ready. Taking the mouthpiece, Master Marlow breathed in and out just like he had been instructed to do before. As soon as the medicine cup was empty, Felix turned off the machine and took it downstairs to thoroughly clean all its parts. Thus, the master was left alone with his thoughts. He desperately wanted to continue pondering on how he could have contracted such a dreadful disease, but he struggled to stay awake enough to do so. The antibiotics were making him drowsy once again, and before he knew it, he succumbed to their overpowering influence and fell fast asleep.

II

For the rest of the first day of his recovery, Master Marlow acquiesced to Felix's wishes and stayed in bed, mainly because he slept for most of the day. However, by the second day, he was already itching to get up, something he knew that Felix would most definitely object to. Part of the reason he was so eager to be back on his feet was simply the nature of his character. The master had always been rather stoic, tough, and independent. Even if he were bleeding to death, he would insist on getting up and doing something. He didn't like to be idle or thought of as an invalid. Another reason was that he had had a rough night. One minute, he felt as hot as a boiler and had to throw off the covers. The next minute, he was shivering as violently as a man having a seizure and had to clamber back under the downy bundles of warmth. It was a constant tug-of-war with the blanket, and no matter which way he tossed and turned, he just couldn't get comfortable. It also didn't help that his brain decided to trigger mini coughing fits every time he was on the verge of falling asleep.

However, the main reason he couldn't sleep was because

of a nagging question that kept poking him in the back of his mind: How had he ended up with pneumonia? It just didn't make any sense. He had never been one to get sick very often, and when he did, he usually just had a minor cold. It was certainly never something as serious as this. Where could it have come from? He hadn't been around anyone at home or the clinic who had been diagnosed with pneumonia, at least, not that he knew of. But perhaps he had come in contact with someone who had the disease and didn't know it. That was a possibility. After all, countless people were carriers of pneumonia-causing bacteria that had detrimental effects on others but not on themselves. Whatever the reason, he had to figure it out.

Early that morning, Felix decided to go ahead and run some errands in town to give the master more time to rest before giving him his morning dose of medicine. He paused in front of the master's room and peeked in at his sleeping figure. The sheets rose and fell peacefully with each breath. His breathing looked and sounded much less laborious than it had before. Satisfied that everything would be fine until he returned, the butler softly pattered downstairs and prepared to leave. As soon as he heard the click of the lock on the front door, Master Marlow opened his eyes from their feigned sleep. This was perfect! With Felix gone, he would be free to get up, move around, and try to piece together this puzzling mystery.

Slowly, he pushed himself up. Such a sudden change in position caused the fluid in his lungs to shift and hinder his breathing. Consequently, he was thrown into a series of ragged and garbled coughs. Each expulsion was so forceful that it looked as if the master were experiencing whip-lash. He doubled over in pain as his eyes began to water. It felt as if all his insides were being ripped away from their connective tissues. However, after hacking into his hand-kerchief for several more excruciatingly long minutes, the rest of his coughs dissipated, and he was able to catch his breath. That first gasp of air was like a soothing balm to his burning lungs, and each successive one helped to cleanse his system. He remained in this meditative position for a long while before he ventured to work his way any further out of bed.

Once he was sure that he had fully recovered (other than a few occasional coughs), he pushed the blankets down and swung his legs over the side of the bed. He shiv-ered as soon as his feet brushed the cool wooden boards. It was cold in the house, or at least, it felt cold to him. He sniffed, his nose beginning to run. Perhaps this wasn't such a good idea after all. Maybe he should just lie down and snuggle back under his cozy blankets and pillows like Felix would want. No, it would be fine. He would just take some of the warmth with him. Leaning over and grabbing an extra blanket folded up at the foot of his bed, Master Mar-low threw it around his shoulders and fastened it around his neck like one of his cloaks. He wrapped the fuzzy fab-ric tightly about himself and instantly felt the comforting heat from the furnace of his body collecting and expanding around him like a protective bubble.

Thus insulated, he planted his feet firmly on the floor and stood. A coldness, like that of a pitcher full of ice water, suddenly poured over his head and dripped down his skin as the blood drained away from his face. The room began to wobble, and fireworks popped in front of his eyes. He was lightheaded. He needed to grab on to something and steady himself before he passed out. Spotting one of the bed posts, he lurched toward it and clung to it like a man adrift at sea, clutching a piece of wood just to stay afloat. He closed his eyes against the spinning bursts of light and took deep shuddering breaths. His whole body quivered along with his heart, and he felt winded and fatigued even though he hadn't done anything strenuous. The master was surprised at how weak he had become. He had only been lying in bed for about two days, and his body was already unaccustomed to being in a vertical position. It truly was amazing to see just how quickly muscles begin to atrophy when not in use.

Finally, his heart rate slowed, and the flashes faded. Tentatively, he opened his eyes. The room was no longer quaking, and neither was he. Everything was steady. Feeling a little of his strength return, the master took a deep breath, wiped off a mustache of clammy sweat that had gathered on his upper lip, and hesitantly released his grip on the post. Nothing happened. He was still standing, so he took a tiny step forward. Still nothing happened. Deciding that he was indeed fit to walk, the master slowly shuffled across the room. However, about halfway to the door, he stopped. He still wasn't quite warm enough. A frigid draft kept breathing down his blanket from around his neck. Making his way over to his closet, he opened its narrow door and rummaged through its dark interior until he pulled out a bright red scarf. He quickly tied it around his neck, and the irksome puffs of air ceased. *Much better,* he thought. Now he was ready. Closing up his closet, he continued to the door of his room, put on his slippers, and scooted out into the hall.

He slowly crept toward his study. Upon opening the door, he immediately began scanning every surface in the room. As long as Felix hadn't taken it to the wash, it should still be in here. It had to be. He squinted into the inky darkness that clouded the room, trying to identify each object he came across. It must have been an overcast morning, for hardly any light leaked in through the cracks of the closed blinds. However, it was enough to guide the master's way. He moved through its grayish glow over to his desk and rested his hands on the back of his leather chair. His desk was a mess! Papers and letters were strewn everywhere as if they had been scattered by a hurricane. His quill tottered out of its inkwell, freckling the table and various papers with blots of ink. The wax from his candle had been allowed to spill over its brass holder, and a thin layer of dust had even begun to settle over everything. Had he really left this place in such disorder the last time he was in here?

He had not realized just how much had been neglected since he had been sick. Oh, well. He would straighten it all out later. Suddenly, something among the disheveled piles caught his attention. Crumpled on the farthest corner of his desk was what appeared to be a wadded-up ball of paper. He moved closer to it. No, it wasn't paper; it was what he had been looking for: the handkerchief that Andrew had given him the night of the dinner. Snatching it up, he hurried out of the room and made his way downstairs. Hopefully, this would give him some answers.

Once he was downstairs, he shuffled through the hall and ducked into the operation room. Pulling out a microscope, he prepared to get to work, when something else caught his attention. One of the napkins from the dinner had been laid haphazardly on the counter. What was it doing in here? The master certainly hadn't put it there. Perhaps Felix had done it. But why? Master Marlow picked up the white cloth and rubbed it between his fingers. It had that same grainy texture on its surface that he had noticed the other night. Initially, the master had thought that Felix had simply over-starched the fabric, but now, he wasn't so sure. It was all rather peculiar. Maybe that was why Felix had brought it in here. Maybe he was going to examine what was on it. However, it seemed that he had never gotten around to it, so the master would do it for him.

Setting the napkin back down, he moved over to the sink and thoroughly washed his hands. Since he was sick and didn't know what he might be dealing with, he also put on a pair of latex gloves and a blue medical mask. He didn't want to risk contaminating himself or his samples any further. Next, he grabbed a pair of tweezers, a pipet, and a small beaker which he filled with water. After placing those items beside the microscope, he sat down and began his investigation.

He started with the napkin. Taking the tweezers, he carefully scraped some of the white powder onto a glass slide and centered it on the microscope. Once it was secure, he adjusted the light and peered through the lens. It took a few turns of the different knobs, but the image finally came into focus. And what the master saw surprised him. It wasn't starch at all; it was tiny specks of white pepper! So that was what had caused him to start sneezing! However, it still didn't explain how he had contracted pneumonia. In fact, it only raised more questions and confusion. Why was it on his napkin? Had Felix accidentally spilled some on it when he was cooking? No. None of those recipes called for white pepper. Besides, the entire napkin was coated in it. That couldn't have happened by accident. It just didn't make any sense. Perhaps whatever he found on the hand-kerchief would help explain things.

Setting his first sample in the sink, he prepared another slide for his second one. He would need water this time. After picking a few flaky samples off the handkerchief, he filled the pipet with water and squeezed a tiny drop, no bigger than a pearl of dew, onto the fragmented substance and gently placed a thin covering over it. He mopped up the excess liquid and positioned it on the microscope. Once it came into focus, the master couldn't believe what he saw. Without heat or a host, they had already decayed signifi-cantly, but he could still clearly discern what those deteri-orated blobs were. They were fragments of pneumococcus, the bacteria that causes pneumococcal pneumonia, a con-tagious form of the disease. Well, that explained it. That's how he became so ill. But…wait. Why were the bacteria *on* the handkerchief? No. No, it couldn't be. It just couldn't.

He lunged over to the incubator but paused in the act of opening its door. His heart pounded in his chest, and his airways constricted. He ripped off his mask, so he could breathe more freely. This was it. Whatever was behind that door would give him his answer. Good or bad. However, he had a sinking feeling in the pit of his stomach that told him that he already knew, but he didn't want to believe it. Trying to push that feeling behind him, he held his breath and forced himself to open the door. His heart seemed to stop beating altogether. *No,* he desperately thought. *It can't be true. Please, tell me that this isn't true.* But it was. The un-mistakable proof was right in front of his eyes. On one of the shelves that held his specimens of bacteria, one of his petri dishes of pneumococcus was missing.

A lightheadedness swept over him once again, and he had to sit down. The master felt sick, not from the illness that he was currently suffering under, but from a new disease that now seeped into his heart. This had to be wrong. There had to be something he wasn't seeing. It must be a terrible nightmare that he would soon awake from…yet…it was the only logical explanation.

Suddenly, the sound of hooves cantering up the drive-way distracted him from his terrible discovery. Felix was back. Quickly, he tossed his mask, gloves, and samples into the trash bin and cleaned off his equipment. Once he had stored everything back in its proper place, he dashed back upstairs. The sound of the lock turning in the door echoed behind him. He had to hurry. Before he knew it, he heard the door open with a creak.

"I'm home, Sir!"

Footsteps rapidly began thumping up the stairs. Franti-cally, the master kicked off his slippers, flung his scarf into his closet, and dove into bed. As soon as he had pulled the cover up and settled his head onto his pillows, Felix poked his head in the doorway.

"Good morning, Sir," he greeted with a cheerful smile. "Did you sleep well?"

The master feared that his voice would give him away since he was still winded from bolting back to his room, so he simply nodded.

"Good. I just got back from running errands in town. Let me finish putting the groceries away, and I'll be right back to give you your morning dose of medicine."

With that, the oblivious butler sauntered back downstairs, and Master Marlow released a huge sigh of relief. He had done it. He had solved the mystery, and Felix was none the wiser. Yet, he suddenly wished that he had not grown any wiser himself.

12

Dear Alvera,

*I never had the chance to tell you this, but thank you
so much for everything you did for me. If it weren't
for you, I probably wouldn't be here right now. I'm
impressed at how well you handled the situation. You
remembered your lessons well. I promise that we will
continue them as soon as I fully recover. As of right
now, I'm happy to say that I am feeling much better,
but I can't wait to be completely well. Felix is about
to drive me absolutely mad! It seems like every five
minutes he comes in to check on me. I can't go anywhere
or do anything without him following me as if he's
my shadow or something. I can't even clear my throat
without causing him alarm! I know he's just trying to
take care of me, but it's still rather irritating. Oh, well.
If I've put up with it for this long, I suppose I can endure it a little longer. Right? Either way, I hope you're
doing much better than I am.*

Master Marlow paused and rested his quill against his chin. He debated whether or not he should tell Alvera about his recent findings. No. It would be wiser to wait. After all, he still wasn't entirely sure who the culprit was. There was no reason to stir up unnecessary fear when the situation was uncertain. Besides, such a serious accusation should not be conveyed by letter in case it should end up in the wrong hands. When the time was right, he would tell Alvera in person, but for right now, he would keep the information to himself.

Having made his decision, the master signed his letter, folded it, and slipped it into an envelope; however, instead of proceeding to write down the proper addresses, he simply stared at the blank face of the envelope and contemplatively slid his fingers over its cream-colored edges. It had been several days since he had heard from Alvera, and he was worried. It wasn't like her. She had always been faithful to write him a letter almost every day. Perhaps her workload at school had increased, robbing her of all her spare time to engage in other activities, or maybe she was simply giving the master extra time to rest and recover without being disturbed by the usual influx of letters. Whatever the reason, he hoped that this letter would trigger some kind of response.

The next day in the afternoon, Master Marlow came downstairs for the first time since he had sneaked out of bed to investigate the cause of his mysterious illness. Felix didn't like the idea, but he would have to get used to it. The master needed to start moving around more in order to build his strength and endurance back up. However, that didn't stop the overbearing butler from fretting over him, for as soon as he had settled himself in one of the cushioned chairs in the den, Felix promptly strutted in front of him and examined him meticulously. The master was already wearing his cloak and a scarf, but upon the butler's insistence, he was also given a blanket, hot tea, and a crackling fire. He tried to protest, but Felix pretended not to hear him. Patting him on the shoulder, he went back to his chores. Irritated, Master Marlow defiantly crossed his arms, slumped grumpily into the cushions, and glowered at the spot where the butler had vanished. He didn't like being treated this way. He wasn't a helpless infant. He was a grown man who was perfectly capable of doing things for himself, even while he was sick. After all, his condition was stable and steadily improving now. He didn't need such intensive care anymore.

A particularly loud pop from the fireplace distracted him from his sulking. The fire was just beginning to blaze through the gnarled heap of logs. Its wispy autumn-colored hands reached out and caressed the master's cheeks, bringing a contented smile to his eyes and lips. He didn't want to admit it, but the golden warmth pulsating from the hearth was just what he needed. The waxing chill of winter creeping into the dry air was affecting his body in its weakened state more than he had realized. Letting the comforting heat melt his icy rage, he relented to Felix's kindness, snuggled deeper under the plush folds of the blanket, grabbed a book off the small mahogany table next to him, and began to read.

A few moments later, he heard the screen in the side

door rattle as it closed. Felix had just come back in from checking the mailbox.

Without lifting his eyes from the pages of his book, the master asked disinterestedly, "Well, what did we get today?"

"Nothing really," he said, flipping through an assortment of bills and flyers. "Unless you're interested in buying a car or knowing how much last month's electric bill was?"

Master Marlow just shook his head. It was just as he thought.

"Wait," Felix corrected. "There *is* something."

The master abruptly looked up and straightened in his chair. Could it be? So soon?

"It looks like a letter from Alvera."

Tossing his book aside, he peeled back the blanket and started pushing himself up. The butler saw his attempt to stand and immediately rushed over to him.

"Oh, Sir! You don't have to get up. Here. I'll bring it to you."

After handing him the letter, Felix stooped down to grab the blanket that had fallen to the floor and draped it back over the master. All the while, Master Marlow stared in awe at the coveted letter he now held in his hands. He couldn't believe it. He hadn't expected a response to arrive this quickly, but he was no less grateful for it. He started to flip it onto its back when something on the face of the envelope caught his attention. A crease formed in the middle of his forehead as he studied it. There was no name above Alvera's address. She always wrote her name before copying down her address. Perhaps she had gotten in a hurry and forgot. Shaking off the strangeness of his discovery, the master turned the envelope over, ripped the flap open, and pulled out the letter. After he unfolded it, however, his initial qualms returned. This wasn't Alvera's handwriting. Something was wrong. If it came from her house but she didn't write it, then who did? With growing trepidation, he began to read.

Dear Mr. Marlow,

This is Anita Levlen, Alvera's mother. I am writing to you on Alvera's behalf. We are all very happy to hear that you are feeling much better, and we pray that you continue to have a quick recovery. Alvera would be telling you all this if she could, but right now, she is also sick with pneumonia. She just came home from the hospital today, but she's still very, very weak. I'm so sorry to have to tell you this, but I knew that you would want to know. Please be praying for her. I'll keep you updated on her condition, and Alvera promises to write to you as soon as she's able. Thank you so much!

In Christ,
Anita Levlen

Both of the master's hands were trembling by the time he got to the end. In fact, they shook so violently that the words on the paper blurred in the flickering light of the fire. Eventually, the letter slipped out of his feeble grasp and fluttered onto his lap, but he didn't seem to notice. If he did, he didn't care. He simply continued to stare at the place where it had been. Hideous phantasms drifted like smoke before his eyes from those ominous words and tormented him with ghastly accusations and whispered lies that he feared contained more truth than falsity, and he allowed their negativity to seep into his mind. Before he knew it, an overwhelming deluge of guilt and grief swelled within his chest, causing a deeper ache than even his illness could produce. It was his fault. All his fault. And he hated himself because of it.

Felix suddenly emerged from dusting in the library. His cheerful grin drooped into a worried frown as soon as he saw the master's troubled face.

"Sir, is something wrong? What is it? What did she say?"

Without looking away from the monstrous visions still dancing before his eyes, he groped for the letter in his lap and forcefully shoved it toward the concerned butler. "Read it."

Tentatively, Felix took the letter and quickly skimmed over its contents. About halfway through, he closed his eyes as a sharp thorn lodged itself in his heart. He understood.

"Oh, Sir. I'm so terribly sorry."

"It's all my fault," came a muffled response.

He looked up. Master Marlow had buried his face in his hands and was shaking his head. Felix leaned closer. A sternness slowly sharpened all his features as he carefully scrutinized the master's hunched figure.

"Wait a minute now. No. No. Don't you do this. You

always do this to yourself, and once it starts, before I know it, you can't sleep, and you stop eating. And those are two things you cannot afford to do right now."

"I don't care."

"Oh, Sir. Don't say that." He clasped one of the master's hands in his own. "Think of Alvera."

"That's all I can think about."

"Well, then, think about what she would say. She would want you to take care of yourself."

"I want her to take care of herself right now."

"She will, but it will be a lot easier for her if she knows that you are doing the same. She needs you, Sir."

"No. I've ruined her life. It would have been better if we had never met."

"Now, Sir. That is simply not true," he said changing his tone and rising to his feet. "Who stitched up her wound from the plane crash and kept her from bleeding to death? Who rescued her from a pack of vicious wolves? Who was there to comfort her when she was in most need of a friend? Who returned her safely to her parents?"

"Who infected her with a deadly disease?"

The master's sardonic remark caused the butler's countenance to falter momentarily, but he quickly regained his firm disposition. "No ... that's ..."

"What are you trying to convince me of?" the master suddenly spat, interrupting him yet again. "That Alvera didn't contract pneumonia from mee?"

The two gazed intensely at each other for a moment before Felix took a deep breath to calm his voice. "Sir, I'm not denying the source; I'm simply denying your assertion of it being your fault. If anything, it's my fault. I'm the one who asked Alvera to help me figure out what was wrong with you. But even if I hadn't, she was already on her way over to see you. She wanted to help you. Because she cares about you."

The master stared at his lap for a long time before softly answering, "I know."

"Besides," Felix continued, "if she had not have been here, I honestly don't think you would have made it through the night."

"I know."

A stone-like silence settled over the room and seemed to petrify everything it touched. The only thing it could not subdue was the fire, which snapped and hissed menacingly as if trying to frighten the unwelcome intruder away. However, it wasn't enough to keep it from penetrating the vulnerable doctor. As he sat brooding in his statuesque repose, he felt its icicle fingers slither and twist their way into the innermost recesses of his soul. They were searching for his greatest weakness. Finally, they found it, still pink and tender from a previous wound, but it was securely sealed away behind a massive lock to protect it while it continued to heal. No matter. They would simply pick it with their needle-like nails. The master felt every painful prick from those miniature daggers, a violation he had felt once before.

Suddenly, the lock broke, and its shattered fragments ripped the tender gash open afresh. An excruciating flash of pain shot through his entire body like a bolt of lightning before being replaced by a saline warmth. It felt like blood pouring from the lacerated edges of his soul and filling up his insides; only, it wasn't blood. The melancholy tide rose higher and higher with each passing second. He wanted to stop it, but he knew that he couldn't. Consequently, it flowed through his words.

"But … I don't want to be the reason … if she should …" He choked on a phlegm-like lump that had suddenly risen up his throat and began wildly coughing. Felix administered several hard blows to his back.

"Oh! please, Sir. Don't think like that. You're getting yourself all worked up for no reason. Listen," he said, kneeling back down and putting an arm around the master's shoulders. "Alvera is a strong girl. Probably much stronger than either of us knows. I'm sure she'll be fine."

"I know," he agreed, his voice still thick with emotion. "I just … I just wish I could go see her myself and make sure she's fine."

"I know, Sir. But you can't. Both of you are far too ill to see each other just yet. You would only be continuing your game of pass it on. Right now, the best thing you can do is exactly what Alvera's mother said: pray. Have faith that everything will be all right, and know that it is not your fault."

The master solemnly nodded.

"Now, I want you to promise me that you will stop blaming yourself for this. Promise me."

Master Marlow thought about the butler's impossible proposition for several prolonged minutes before compromising with, "I'll try."

"No. No. A promise has to be in the absolute affirmative."

"All right," he groaned. "I promise."

"Now, look me in the eye and say it," Felix said, leaning even closer.

"Felix."

"All right. All right," he relented while backing away. "Very good."

13

The master tried to keep his promise. He really did try, but even with the frequent updates from Anita, he just couldn't shake the burdensome feeling of guilt off his shoulders. And it wasn't just the guilt he felt over Alvera's condition. That first letter had stirred up deeper levels of regret and remorse than anyone could have ever known, and they had secretly been bothering him since his visit with his mother. So far, he had been able to push them back every time they had tried to surface, for he had had his job at the clinic and chores around the house to distract his troubled mind. But now that he was forced to take it easy and another catastrophe had shattered his life, their surge had become too powerful for him. Every day those tumultuous feelings were gaining ground, feeding the emotional milkshake swirling nauseatingly in his stomach. He didn't have the strength to fight them off any longer, and he was tired of struggling in this sickening pit of depression. He needed relief, and he knew where he needed to go to find it.

* * *

The stub of a candle glowed dimly in the midst of a pool of wax that threatened to drown it at any moment. Its feeble flame flickered to the scratching of a quill hurriedly scribbling on a small scrap of paper. All was silent except for this rodent-like gnawing, but suddenly, it ceased as the ink-soaked tip jerked to a stop. Master Marlow lifted his head and listened intently. He thought he had heard something. No. There was nothing but the deathly silence of darkness. He bent back over his work and continued writing. When he finished, he carefully folded the note, shoved it in one of his coat pockets, stuck a letter in the other pocket, and finally put the dying candle out of its misery. He looked over at the window. It was just beginning to grow light out. Perfect.

Adjusting his scarf, he slowly crossed the nearly imperceptible study floor so as not to trip over anything. His fingers blindly yet quietly groped about for the doorknob. As soon as they brushed its smooth metal surface, they firmly wrapped themselves around it and made as if to turn it, but the master stopped their progress to listen once again. Nothing. All was still silent. He cautiously proceeded. Opening the door wide enough for his head to stick out, he scanned the shadowy hallway like an owl watching for even the slightest tremble of a mouse's whisker. Nope. All was clear, so he slipped the rest of his body into the hall and headed downstairs. At the bottom, he froze, ninja-like, and examined the ghostly silhouettes of the furniture looming up from the depthless floor. Aside from their grotesque forms, everything seemed normal. Nothing was missing or out of place. No mysterious figure lurked in any hidden corner, and no one occupied any of the chairs except for the darkness, which was quickly dissipating in morning's purifying light. He was indeed alone. Still, he could not let his guard down, so as noiselessly as he could, he stealthily tiptoed through the kitchen toward the side door. His heart beat louder and faster in anticipation as he drew nearer to the door. He couldn't believe it! Just a few feet now. He was going to make it! A few centimeters. He was almost there! He reached for the handle.

"Where do you think you're going?"

The accusatory question detonated the silence like a bomb, hurling the master backward with its shockwaves. Still alarmed, he jerked his entire body around and was met with the butler's slender figure, silhouetted by the warm glow of the oil lamps, glaring down at him like a vulture from the top of the stairs. Master Marlow squeezed his eyes shut and grimaced. He had been caught. *Of all the mornings for Felix to be up extra early, he had to pick this one,* he thought, irritated. The soft thumps of rapidly approaching feet interrupted his frustration. He would have to think quickly. Perhaps there was still a way he could play this off. Calming his shaken nerves, Master Marlow managed to banish the guilt from his eyes just as Felix stopped a few feet in front of him.

"Well?" he demanded in an even more unforgiving tone.

"I'm taking a letter to the mailbox."

Felix stared directly into the master's eyes before glancing down at his feet. Putting a hand on his hip, he looked back up with a raised eyebrow. "In your riding boots?"

Master Marlow instinctively looked down and shuffled uncomfortably. *Ugh!* He had forgotten about the boots. Closing his eyes, he hung his head even further. There was no fooling Felix now.

The butler waited for an answer for several painfully long minutes. Seeing that he would get none, he held out the hand that was not firmly planted on his hip. "Let me see 'the letter.'"

After a momentary pause, the master reluctantly reached into his left pocket, pulled out the envelope, and laid it in Felix's expectant palm. Bringing it toward himself and holding it with both hands, he warily examined it, his eyes constantly darting back and forth between the letter and Master Marlow the entire time. He flipped it over and over and over again before finally holding it up to the light. He squinted at its contents. Convinced that it was indeed a legitimate letter, he looked back at the master and laid it on the counter.

"Here," he said walking past him and grabbing his coat off the wall. "*I'll* put it in the mailbox for you."

"Fine," the master acquiesced as he turned to leave. "But I'm still going out."

"Oh, no, you're not," Felix countered, sliding between the master and the door. "I'm sorry, Sir, but I cannot allow you to go out there. Do you know how cold it is? Besides, the last time you went out this door I found you sprawled out on your back."

"When I was sick."

"Oh? So, you don't think you still are?"

"I didn't say that."

"Then, you're affirming that you are."

"No, I'm not."

Master Marlow suddenly backed away and coughed into his arm. When he looked back at Felix, a knowing look rested on the butler's stern face.

"You just did."

His words were sparks lighting the master's short fuse. He could feel their goading fire crackling beneath his skin. It was lava, ready to spew from his mouth at any moment. He only needed one word to reduce anyone who stood in his way into a pile of ash. All he had to do was fight back, but instead, he simply turned away in defeat. There was no point in arguing. Felix wouldn't listen. He just didn't understand. Besides, such a confrontation would only cause more hurt, and the master had already had enough of that.

An unexpected wave of despair extinguished his anger. His hurt. It was surfacing again. *No. Not here. Not now. Not yet.* But it was too late. He felt it all with a force he had never experienced before. All the tears he had never shed. All the words he had never said. All his wounds that had never been mended. All the lies that never ended. Remorse, guilt, insecurity, doubt, grief, pain. They all tore mercilessly at his weary heart. He had been so close. So close to being free. But he had failed.

If only Felix could understand. How much he was suffering! If only he could tell him, but he could never do that. Felix could never know the full extent of his pain. It would be too great a burden for him to bear. It was already too much for the master. He couldn't take it any longer, yet somehow, he was still holding on. Perhaps he was simply meant to struggle, forever tormented by the possibility of relief, for it was ever tantalizingly near, but never to be attained.

The pressure of it all now began to squeeze his heart, wringing every last sorrow-drenched tear from it. Master Marlow felt as if he were a cracked water pipe ready to burst. He knew he couldn't keep it in, so he simply took a sharp breath and held it to steady the stormy waters for the time being. Felix must have heard him, for he postponed his trip to the mailbox and walked over to the grieving doctor instead.

He put a hand on his shoulder and sighed. "Listen, Sir," he began in his usually gentle voice. "I'm only being so strict and doing all these things that you consider irksome because I care about you. I know you're tired of being cooped up at home. I know you want to get back out there, but you're not ready yet. You're still too weak. Especially with winter having already set in. I…I just don't want to see you go under again. You'll be able to get out soon enough, but for now, just rest a little longer."

He smiled hopefully as he waited for a response, but Master Marlow just kept silently staring down at the tips of his boots as if Felix weren't even there. Worry erased his optimism.

"Sir, please, look at me."

Ever so slightly, the master raised his head and slowly lifted up his eyes. It was all he could do; otherwise, he feared that he would lose his grip on the storm that was still violently struggling against him. Felix met his pitiful puppy dog gaze. He looked absolutely miserable. More so than the butler had seen him in a long time. His face softened with even more compassion.

"I hate seeing you like this." He forced another smile. "Cheer up. It's going to be all right."

Patting him on the shoulder, Felix slowly moved away and headed outside. The garden door clattered noisily like a bunch of chains against the frame. Master Marlow just stared at it even after its shimmying ceased. This house had become his prison once again. He'd never wriggle out of its ensnaring bars. Suddenly, his breathing grew heavy, and his eyes venomous as a passionate flame swelled within his chest. No. He would not be submissive or restrained any longer. Not after he had come so far. No matter what it took, he was determined to break his strangling bonds. He was determined to finally be free.

So, as soon as Felix was out of sight, he dashed out the front door and jogged around back. There, he found the horses still asleep in their stalls. Frank, alternately snoring and grinding his teeth, was propped against one of the wooden walls while Obsidian quietly lay curled on a pile of hay. However, when he heard the soft click of the latch on the fence, Obsidian immediately rose to his hooves, shook the debris from his mane, and nickered a friendly welcome to his approaching master. (Frank snored on.) His star shone almost as brightly as his ebony eyes did with love and devotion.

Even though depression weighed his spirit down, it couldn't keep the master's lips from curling into a slight smile at that sight. Such loyalty. He reached out and rubbed the silky neck stretched before him. Obsidian responded with various subdued nickers, whinnies, and whistles and by nuzzling his master's hair. Just then, something inside the master broke, and when it did, his smile shattered along with it.

"Oh, Sid."

He cradled the massive head in his hands and pressed his forehead to the little white star. It seemed to pulsate like the warm beating of a heart against his skin. He closed his eyes. Obsidian leaned in with an equally gentle pressure and did the same. The two remained in this intimate bond for several blissful minutes. An inexplicable peace washed over Master Marlow, and in that moment, a solitary drop of rain fell from one of his eyes. Indeed, it wasn't much, but to the doctor, it felt as if one-thousand drops of sorrow had already been drained from his billowing cloud. What relief! It felt cool, weightless, and …fuzzy?

The master opened his eyes just as Obsidian finished rubbing his muzzle against his cheek, wiping the remainder of his tear away. He looked incredulously at his faithful companion. It was as if he were trying to say, "Don't cry. You have to be strong." He was right. The problem was that the master had thought that he was alone and that he had to be strong on his own. But he didn't. And he wasn't alone.

He sighed and stroked Obsidian's velvety head. "Felix won't understand, but I need you to take me somewhere."

Inside, Felix hummed away while scrubbing a pile of dishes he had left in the sink the night before. He abruptly stopped as the rumble of hooves disrupted his melody.

His eyes widened. *No*, he thought, trying to reassure him-self. *He wouldn't.* The rumbling grew louder and rounded the house. *He would.* Dropping the dish he was holding back in the sink, the butler frantically scrambled toward the front door.

"Of all the foolhardy…"

He yanked the door open and dashed onto the porch, and there, in all his defiant glory, was Master Marlow astride his dazzling steed.

"SIR!"

Spotting the overbearing butler, the master instantly dug his heels into Obsidian's sides. As they galloped away, he reached into his right pocket and threw its contents to the ground. Felix ignored this diversion and continued to pursue, wildly waving the dish towel he was still holding in his hand.

"STOP! PLEASE! COME BACK!"

It was no use. The two escapees had already disappeared over the hill in a cloud of dust. For several minutes, Fe-lix just stood in the middle of the front yard, helpless and distraught. He almost didn't believe what he had just wit-nessed. What was he to do?

Realizing that no matter how long he stared into the dispersing plume of dirt he couldn't bring them back, he worriedly crossed his arms and reluctantly trudged back toward the house. Millions of thoughts raced through his head, but none of them were coherent enough to form a plan. They only left him more scattered and unsure than he was before. If only he had an answer!

Suddenly, something out of the corner of his eye caught

his attention. It was the item the master had tossed from his pocket. He picked it up. It was a small scrap of paper that had been strapped to a rock. Removing it from its weight, he slowly unfolded the crinkled slip. It was a note! With a spark of hope revitalizing his amber eyes, Felix eagerly began to read. It said:

Felix
I'm going to my mother's.
Don't follow me.
I'll be back later.
—Malchus

His mouth fell open as he stared at the maddening sentences. Was this supposed to make him feel better? Pressing the paper to his chest, he looked up at the sky and whispered in a frightened voice, "Dear God! Please, protect him!"

14

The crisp air whistled in their ears like a chorus of birds as they galloped across the fiery countryside. The master's scarf flapped like a pair of cardinal wings behind him. It felt as if they were flying. Flying far away from all their troubles. He closed his eyes and stuck his face into the frosty stream. It was refreshing, invigorating. Obsidian also reared his majestic head just as eagerly and gulped the icy wind by the liter. Each energizing breath fueled every fiber of his body. His nostrils flared a little wider, and his lungs pumped a little faster. His electrified muscles surged with adrenaline, making every stroke of his hooves more powerful than before and every leap stretch a little further. He seemed to have missed the thrill of the unbridled race as much as the master had. It truly was liberating, not just for the mind, but also for the adventurous spirits of both man and wild stallion. Unfortunately, it ended all too soon as they came upon the town, and they were resigned to a peaceful canter for the rest of their journey.

Just as morning reached its zenith, they trotted into the driveway of his mother's house. Master Marlow pulled up on the reins, stopping Obsidian just inside the fence. He stared at the blinding white building ahead. Its boards sparkled like snow in the radiant sun, but they didn't fill him with the same serenity that such a scene normally would. Instead, they reminded him of why he was there. He suddenly wished that he wasn't. Then again, he would rather face his mother than Felix at that point. Besides, he might be uncomfortable now, but he would feel so much better once it was all over.

With a sigh, he slid off Obsidian's back and led him over to a tree in the shade. As he finished tying the reins around the trunk, a sharp blast of wind swept across the yard and sliced right through the master's scarf and coat. He wrapped his arms tightly around his waist and shivered. It wasn't that cold out, but the ride over must have chilled his body more than he had realized. A forceful nudge to his back caught him off guard and sent him stumbling forward. Once he regained his footing, he turned and found Obsidian scanning him with his coal-black eyes. They were filled with concern. He smiled, walked over to him, and petted him reassuringly on the head.

"I know. It's ok."

The stallion snorted. He wasn't convinced, but he let his master go anyway. Nevertheless, before he settled himself down to nibble on some tufts of grass, he eyed him watchfully as he walked the rest of the way up the gravel driveway.

When he reached the door, Master Marlow immediately rang the doorbell. He couldn't hesitate. Not this time. A few seconds later, his mother appeared.

"Malchus?" she said with apparent surprise. "What are you doing here? Are you all right? I heard you were ill."

"I was, but I'm much better now."

She scrutinized his face. "But you still look so pale."

"I always look pale."

She gave him a look before smiling and shaking her head. "You know what I mean." Opening the door a little wider, she stepped to the side. "Well, come on in out of the cold. Let's continue our visit inside."

Agatha waited for her son to come in, but he didn't budge. He just couldn't. Not until he knew. As discreetly as possible, he peeked further into the interior of the house. His mother noticed and understood.

"Don't worry. Your brothers aren't here. You can come on in."

The master still didn't move. *What are you doing?* he yelled at himself. *Just tell her!* But the words wouldn't come. He had suddenly become bashful and indecisive. Blood rushed to his cheeks. Lowering his head, he wrung his hands behind his back and twisted his foot into the ground. "Well, uh…actually, Mother…I was hoping…we could go for a walk," he began doggedly. "It's not too cold out. In fact, it's actually rather nice."

Agatha's countenance changed as she cocked her head slightly to the side and examined her son. He was acting exceedingly strange. Stranger than he had at his previous visit.

"Please?"

His feeble plea startled her, and she finally relented.

"All…all right. Just let me get my shawl, and I'll be right out."

As soon as she was ready, the two began their ambling trek around the yard, close to the wooded perimeter. It didn't provide much of a barrier anymore, for most of the trees had already lost all of their leaves. Their bleached ribs created perfect channels for the wind to funnel through. A few languishing skeletons attempted to stifle the howling gales, but even their tawny cloaks, already patched with persimmon and scarlet, were becoming increasingly threadbare and ragged with winter's chaffing hands. Yet, they were not mourning their inevitable defeat. None of nature was. Even in its death, it still strove to protect and encourage every living creature with its ever-radiant smile. Bony fingers stretched out to hold the flitting sparrows. Their warbling songs blended with the whistling of the wind. The grass, overly tanned by multiple morning frosts, crunched brittlely beneath the strollers' feet, yet it glittered like countless grains of sand in the golden rays of the sun. It was almost warm enough to be a cool day at the beach.

Agatha imagined herself there on the shore, drifting barefoot down those shifting slopes toward the gently foaming sea, feeling every sun-tanned speck squish between her toes. She could almost smell the salty spray. She was glad her son had talked her into coming out. It truly was a deliciously beautiful day.

She looked over at him to see if he was reveling in the mellow weather as much as she was. Her hopeful eyes were instantly shadowed by the moth-eaten shade that he was walking in. It looked as if Master Marlow were enveloped in a storm cloud. His hands were shoved all the way down into the bottom of his coat pockets. His shoulders were slumped forward, causing him to appear even more hunch-backed than usual, and his head still drooped toward the ground. He was also keeping his distance. However, it was his eyes that intrigued her the most.

Turning away, she continued to walk on in silence for a few more paces before quietly commenting, "Your eyes are dim."

Her voice seemed to echo from miles away. None of her words were intelligible. However, once their noise pricked his ears, Master Marlow partially awoke from his reverie and jerked his head confusedly toward his mother. "What?"

"Your eyes. Whenever something's troubling you, they get this distant, foggy, far-away look in them."

"Oh." He shrugged as if to dismiss her.

Agatha abruptly stopped and turned toward her son in a way that demanded his attention. He did the same and looked her fully in the face for the first time since they had been outside. It felt as if she could see right through him. He didn't like feeling so vulnerable and exposed, but there was no escape. Her penetrating eyes seemed to nail his feet to the ground.

"Malchus," she began in a gentle yet serious tone, "I don't believe you asked me to walk with you just to enjoy this unusually warm winter day. You can't fool me. I'm your mother. I raised you. Now, just tell me. What's bothering you?"

Another painful blush stung the master's cheeks, causing him to avert his gaze yet again. He stared absentmindedly at the grass for a few moments before closing his eyes and taking a deep breath. This is why he had come. It was time. He had to stop running.

"Mother…" he swallowed and forced himself to look at her. "Do…do you remember the day I left?"

"Yes, of course I remember."

He hung his head. "I'm sorry."

"Sorry? Whatever for?"

"For that being the last memory you have of me. I wasn't thinking about you or anyone else that day. I was only thinking about myself. What I thought was best for me. And I know I hurt you. I never meant to, but I did. That's all I ever seem to do. I didn't even say goodbye. I'm just such a selfish, impulsive, unstable…" He tried to think of an even more odious way to describe himself but couldn't. Instead, he let out a defeated sigh. "I'm sorry. Please, forgive me."

"Oh, Malchus. That's what has been bothering you?"

He nodded.

She drew closer. "My dear boy. Please, don't be so hard on yourself. It's all right."

They resumed walking.

"I was never angry or upset with you. Yes, it did hurt a little at first, but I understood why you left."

Master Marlow looked at her with surprise. She saw his wonder out of the corner of her eye and proceeded to explain. "I wasn't oblivious even though I acted like it. I heard and saw how our family treated you. I wanted to confront your father about it, but…I can't say that I ever did. I always let my fear get in the way." She paused. "Don't get me wrong. I loved your father, but I was also afraid of him. He had such a terrible temper. I never knew what he might do when he was in one of his rages, so … I remained silent to protect myself." Another pause. "I should have put you first. I should have stood up for you, but I didn't. And for that, I'm the one who should be apologizing."

"No."

"Yes."

"Mother, I know it was tough for you. It was tough for all of us. You did the best you could. You were a wonderful mother to me."

She gave him a grateful smile tinged with sadness. "I could have done better."

"We all could have."

Silence fell between them like a void, but it was quickly filled by the playful breeze. It whispered in their ears and rippled beneath their clothes, urging them to continue. Agatha was the first to consent.

"Well, everything happens for a reason, including your leaving home. And from what I've seen, I honestly believe that it was the best thing for you."

The master's lightened spirit was instantly weighed back down by another overcast sky. "I'm not so sure that it was."

His mother detected the subtle change in his voice and looked at him with concern. "What do you mean?"

He hesitated. "Mother, I didn't tell you during our first visit, but … after that horrible article in the newspaper was published about me, I … isolated myself from society for nearly twenty years."

She stopped again and stared at him with gaping mouth

and wide eyes. They glistened like two pools of mercury in the sun as if she were about to cry. "Oh, Malchus! I'm so sorry! If only I had known..."

"No one could have known," he interjected. "I never told anyone but Felix. It was just him and me for the longest time." Slowly, he turned his face toward the sun and closed his eyes. He remembered the loneliness. How its icy claws had bound him so. How miserable he had been before love had thawed his chains and illuminated his darkened heart with a single touch. It had warmed his entire being just as the caressing rays were doing to his pallid skin right then. He smiled at the recollection and continued, "But then Alvera came into my life, and everything changed. She helped me become a better man, Mother. The man you see standing before you today. Before, I was so closed, depressed, bitter, and angry with the world. I almost let it destroy me altogether, but Alvera reminded me that I didn't have to let it. There will always be cruel people in the world, but it doesn't matter what they think. It only matters what you think of yourself. I've learned to love myself just the way God made me. To see myself the way He does, and, I guess, the way you've always seen me."

They smiled lovingly at each other before walking on.

"I guess you were in need of a doctor just as much as she was," Agatha said.

The master's smile widened. "Yes."

"Well, then, I'm very thankful she showed up when she did. Otherwise, I may never have seen my son again." She paused and became contemplative. "But you know, Malchus, you're not the only one who struggled. Your brother, Michael, did too."

Master Marlow listened attentively.

"I'll never forget it. It was just a few days after you left. I was sitting in the den crocheting when he walked up to me and asked why you had left. I had never seen him look so depressed before. As gently as I could, I told him that I believed you left simply to start a new life in the world. He was silent for a moment, but then—Oh, Malchus! —he just burst into tears. He was afraid that you had left because of him."

"No," he said shaking his head. "I mean, it wasn't just Michael; it was our whole family."

"I know. I tried to reassure him that it wasn't his fault. He just felt so badly about the way he had treated you. And I don't think he ever meant to be that way, the poor dear. Being the youngest had its vices. Everyone around him was a role model, and since most of what he heard and saw came from your brother and father, those were the habits and attitudes he mimicked. But that's all they ever were. Parroted words and actions. He never took them to heart. I'm just glad that he finally realized his mistakes and that you two were able to resolve your differences."

"Me too."

They rounded the back of his mother's property before she broke the silence again.

"So how are you and Andrew getting along?"

It felt as if his mother had just thrown him a curve ball. The master would have to answer this question very carefully. He couldn't tell her about the dinner party fiasco.

As far as she knew, everything had gone well. And he certainly couldn't tell her any of his secret knowledge. It would only make things worse. Obviously, she had noticed more at their first visit than he had realized, so basing his answer off that information, he simply said, "We're not."

Her hopefulness faded. "I'm so sorry, Malchus." She laid a comforting hand on his shoulder. However, she quickly withdrew it and clenched both hands into fists as an unexpected burst of anger empowered her frail body. "Ooo! That boy! When will he grow up? I had so hoped that he would have given up all this childish nonsense by now, but …" She released the rest of her frustration with a sigh. The tension in her muscles visibly relaxed. "Perhaps now that you're back in his life, he will realize the damage he's done and want to change."

Master Marlow thought it best not to answer that. However, it did get him thinking about something else.

"Mother?"

"Yes, Dear?"

"Did … Father ever change towards me?"

"Oh, Malchus," she sighed, "I wish I could tell you for certain, but I can't. Your father was just set in his ways and … well … stubborn. Very stubborn. It was his way or no way. Once he decided his opinion on something, it rarely ever changed. However, when he saw the article about you that said you had become the number one surgeon in all of England, I saw something in his eyes that I had never seen before. He never showed it, but I think deep down, he was proud of you."

The master couldn't speak, for a lump had risen in his

throat and kept rising. His father. The imposing figure that had always filled him with so much dread as a child. The overly critical monarch who had both silently and verbally judged his offspring's every move. His most abusive monster lurking in the shadows. *He* was proud of his deformed son. Yes, his mother had previously told him that his whole family was proud of his accomplishments, but to know that his father was proud of him *individually*, meant so much more. It was what every little boy strove for. To earn his father's approval. To feel valued in his eyes. To hear those four powerful words: I'm proud of you.

Master Marlow repeated them over and over in his head as if they were a working needle and thread, and slowly, they began to mend one of the many holes that had eaten away at his heart for so long. Filling it. Healing it. Healing his entire being like warm broth. He could feel its steamy elixir trickling through his veins, soothing every wound it touched, fueling the furnace of his core, and warming all his extremities. He felt whole for once. It was a wonderful feeling, but it wasn't complete. He needed closure. However, in order to get that closure, he would have to sacrifice the comforting glow pulsating within him at that moment, and he wasn't sure if he wanted to do that. He finally had pleasure; did he really want to return to the pain? He didn't, but he had to know. He reminded himself that he wouldn't feel better until he knew. Besides, by facing his pain, he would attain riches that pleasure could never afford: true peace and joy.

Taking a deep breath to steady his nerves and brace

himself for the worst, he turned his head toward his mother and cautiously asked, "Mother, how did Father die?"

He almost regretted asking as he watched her silently fold her hands in front of her. She wouldn't even look in his direction as she quietly said, "I'd rather not say."

His curiosity mounted. "Why not?"

This time, she ignored him altogether. He couldn't take it. Picking up his pace, he stepped a few feet in front of his mother, blocking her path. She could have easily walked around him, but instead, she simply stopped and waited patiently. Master Marlow strained to catch her downcast eyes. "Please, Mother. Please, tell me. I want to know. I need to know."

After contemplating the earnestness in his voice for several minutes, she finally looked up, but eyed him warily. "Well…if I do tell you…Malchus…will you promise me that you won't blame yourself for what happened?"

He stared into her soul-searching eyes. He wondered what they saw. A broken man? A wayward son? Or just an insecure and frightened little boy? It didn't matter. At that moment, all they really wanted was his word.

Without breaking their connection, he nodded and said, "Yes, I promise."

Closing her eyes, she sighed and continued forward. "All right. Well, not too long after Michael started college, your father went to the doctor for his yearly physical. Everything came back normal except for his blood results. The doctor said that he would have to run further tests to verify exactly what he had found, but as soon as he knew, he would let him know. It was nothing to be too worried about, I thought. This kind of thing happened to people all the time. It had to be just an imbalance of sorts. Probably from all those fatty steaks your father liked to eat.

"A few days later, he received a phone call. It was the doctor. I figured that Robert would argue with the results like he always did, but instead, he remained very silent throughout the whole conversation. Not one complaint or disagreement came from his lips. Just a few yeses and I sees. It wasn't like him. So, when he had hung up, I asked him what the doctor had said, but he just looked at me and said, 'It's nothing. I'm fine.' But I knew he was lying. Something was wrong. Day after day I pressed him for an answer, but he would say nothing more. Days turned into weeks, weeks into months, and months into years. He still refused to say anything about the phone call. He also stopped going to the doctor even for his yearly physicals. That's when I really started to worry about him. He was avoiding something, and I soon found out what it was.

"Your father had just gotten home late from work one night, and instead of going to recline in the den like he normally did, he went straight back to our bedroom. When he still had not come out after several minutes, I decided to go check on him. I found him leaned over, sitting on the edge of the bed. He had taken off his shirt, revealing a massive lump protruding between his shoulder blades. It looked like a goose egg trying to hatch out of his back. The first word that popped into my mind was 'cancer,' and it terrified me. I immediately confronted him about it and urged him to go to the doctor, but he just waved it off like all the times before and refused to listen. There was no reasoning with him. It was as if he didn't care anymore.

"Well, I wasn't just about to sit back and watch your father slowly allow himself to die. If he wasn't going to do anything about his condition, I would. So, I called your brothers and told them about the situation, and the three of us started looking for a doctor. After calling around for several months, we still couldn't find anyone who could help. Either their wait lists were too long, or they weren't qualified to perform such a dangerous surgery. I was beginning to lose hope, for by that time, your father's mass had grown considerably and was beginning to affect his health. He was constantly in pain and could barely walk. His vision would blur, his speech would slur, and sometimes, when it was really bad, he would become greatly disoriented. I often feared that it was too late. That we had run out of time. But just when we were about to give up, Michael remembered the article about you in the paper. He figured that if anyone could help Robert, you could. So, I called the clinic where you were working and asked specifically for you, but the nurse on the phone told me that you were no longer there. I asked her if she knew where you had gone, but she told me that no one, not even the clinic, knew. All she could tell me was that you had mysteriously left work one day and never returned. It was as if you had simply disappeared. Well, that had been our last hope, but it wouldn't have mattered anyway. A few days later, your father passed away."

Master Marlow couldn't see where he was going, but he didn't care. His eyes were too full of those terrible memories, old and new. But even they became clouded with the steam of hot tears that began to scald his eyes. He struggled to keep them back. Why had he left? Why hadn't he held out just a little longer? He could have had a real father for the first time, but instead, he was left with less than he had before. He had worked so hard to make him proud, only to fail him in the end. He would forever be haunted by the fact that the last thing his father might have remembered about him was that he hadn't been there when he had needed him the most. His voice was filled with bitter passion as he spoke. "It's all my fault. I was such a fool!"

Agatha stopped and gently reprimanded her son. "Now, now, Malchus. You promised me that you wouldn't blame yourself. It is not your fault."

"But it is. I could have saved him."

"Malchus, there's no way you could have known."

"But I should have." He gave a gruff sigh that sounded more like a growl. "If only I hadn't let my hurt and anger get the best of me."

"Malchus, listen. Even if you had still been at the clinic at the time, I don't think your father would have made it. His cancer had already spread to the rest of his body."

"You don't know that for sure." He paused, taking deep breaths to compose himself, but each one was shakier than the last. His lips trembled and his words faltered as he continued. "I…I could have saved him. Maybe…if I had…I…I…could have…resolved things…I…wish…I…"

Mrs. Marlow couldn't stand to see her son struggling, so before he completely stumbled and broke down, she went to him and wrapped him tightly in her feeble arms. "Shhh…shhh," she soothed as she rocked him and stroked his hair. "It's all right. It's in the past, and no matter how much we want to, we cannot change it. We can only learn from it. I know you wanted to make things right, Malchus, but you can't always fix everything. Your care and compassion show that you loved your father, and beneath his many layers of severity, I know that he loved you too. He just didn't know how to show it. He was always too concerned with how the world looked at his family from the outside to really appreciate the beauty within."

For several more minutes, mother and son stayed in this cradled position, the wind swaying along with them.

"Are you all right now?" Agatha asked after releasing him.

He nodded.

She peered up at him. "What is it? Something's still bothering you. I can see it."

Embarrassment violently flushed the master's cheeks. It was true. He had been comforted, but he still had one more question that wouldn't leave him alone. He was pretty sure he knew the answer, but…

"Mother?"

"Yes?"

He squirmed as if a snake had just slithered down his back. "I was wondering…if…I mean…well, uh…I…"

"Yes?" she urged.

"Did…did you…" He rubbed the sweat off his palms, swallowed the lump that was causing him to stutter, took a deep breath, and blew through the rest of his sentence like a radio announcer spitting out the detailed information at the end of a commercial. "Did you ever have a deep sense of compassion or emotional attachment towards me?"

At first, she just stared at him as if he had lost his mind, but after a few minutes of sorting through his bumbling gibberish, she understood.

"Malchus, are you trying to ask me if *I* ever loved you?"

He nodded sheepishly.

She sighed. "My dear boy. I'm so sorry. You honestly get this from me and your father. I've always had a difficult time expressing how I feel, and I'll admit that I wasn't the most affectionate mother. But please don't doubt me when I say this." She took him by the hands and looked him in the eye. "I have always and will always love you."

"I love you too, Mother." He stared at her for a moment longer before abruptly pulling away. "I'm sorry. I…I never meant to doubt you. I just…"

"Wanted to hear it?"

He looked up, surprised yet again.

A wisdom-filled smile glowed on his mother's face. "I know. After all, you're not the first one to ask me. Michael did too." Her smile broadened. "Even though you two look so different from each other, you really are very much alike."

"Yes," the master agreed with a chuckle. Dear Michael! He had only seen and spoken with him twice now, but he was already growing quite fond of him. He couldn't wait to get to know his brother even more. He looked back at his mother. "Thank you for letting me talk with you. I feel much better."

"I'm glad. Just know that you can always come to me."

He smiled. A true smile. Suddenly, a gust of wind threatened to knock them over. Both wrapped their winter coverings more tightly about themselves, but it wasn't enough to completely shield out the frigid blast. It slipped beneath Master Marlow's scarf and shocked his lungs, sending him into a coughing fit.

"Forgive me…the wind," he sputtered between hacks. "I suppose I'm not as well as I thought I was. Perhaps we should go back inside."

"Yes," agreed his mother, putting an arm around his waist and leading him toward the house, "let's get you warm. I'll make us some nice hot tea."

"That sounds lovely."

15

Just as he had expected, the master received an earful from Felix when he returned, but it was worth it. No amount of lecturing or reprimands could dampen his spirit. The burden that he had been carrying around for so long had fallen off his shoulders with a great thud, liberating him from the very ground on which he stood. He was free, finally free, and could now focus on more important things.

Alvera had almost fully recovered, as her mother had informed him, and had resumed her correspondence with him. He appreciated the time and effort Anita had taken to write to him on Alvera's behalf, but it just didn't compare to hearing from Alvera herself. He had missed her dainty cursive with all its peculiar jots and inflections unfurling like ribbons across the page. He could almost hear her sweet voice whispering to him in each stroke of her pen. In her most recent letter, she told him that she hoped to be able to visit him soon. At the bottom, she had sketched a little cartoon of a girl looking longingly out a window. The master smiled at it before pushing it to the side. Sliding a fresh sheet of paper in front of him, he dipped his quill in ink and began to write. Perhaps she would be able to visit even sooner than she thought.

* * *

It was evening. Master Marlow sat in the library. Felix had just finished clearing away the dishes from dinner and had headed upstairs, giving the master plenty of solitude to read. The distant ticking of a clock and the occasional turning of a page were the only sounds that penetrated the peaceful silence. Suddenly, they were joined by a soft knocking at the front door. Marking his place, the master set his book aside and rose from his chair.

"I'll get it, Felix," he called as he entered the hall. No response. He must not have heard him. No matter. Master Marlow continued toward the door. However, as soon as he opened it, he was quite taken aback.

"Don't laugh," said a muffled voice.

It sounded like Alvera…somewhere. All he could see were her eyes. The rest of her body looked as if it had been stuffed inside several marshmallows. A pair of rubber boots were squeezed over multiple layers of pants that overflowed their tops. A puffed-up jacket kept her arms from coming all the way down and nearly swallowed her mitten-covered hands. It also looked as if it were about to burst its zipper. A scarf was tightly wound about her neck and had been pulled over her mouth and nose. Earmuffs stuck out like dandelion fluff from the sides, and to top off the ridiculous ensemble, a knitted winter hat with a snowball bobbing at the end sat snugly on her head, nearly obscuring her eyes.

The master tried not to make a face as she waddled over the threshold. As soon as she was inside, she immediately began removing her burdensome gear.

"What is all this?" he asked as he helped her peel off some of the layers.

She gave an irritated sigh and rolled her eyes. "My mom said that I could only come over if I bundled up."

"For what? Antarctica?"

She giggled. "I guess I finally understand how you've been feeling with Mr. Felix."

He smiled. "Well, other than that, how have you been?"

"Much better."

Their little reunion was cut short by the sound of hurried footsteps thumping down the stairs. "Sir, did you call me?" Felix stopped when he reached the bottom. "Alvera? What are you doing here?"

"She came to visit," the master answered for her.

"Well, I wish I would have known. I would have … wait." He looked suspiciously from one of them to the other. "You two were in on this together?"

Neither said a word.

Hurt mingled with outrage overshadowed the butler's face as he addressed Master Marlow. "I can't believe you. Endangering her like this. It's one thing for you to go galivanting off, but her … She shouldn't be going out in her condition. I'm surprised her mother even agreed to it."

"Mr. Felix, it's ok. I'm …"

"Especially when she's not wearing nearly enough layers."

"Not enough? Any more and I wouldn't even be able to stand!"

"Well, if you can't stand, then you shouldn't come."

Alvera's eyes grew round with surprise. She had never seen Felix so stern before, but he was right. An overwhelming guilt pierced her heart and weighed her head down. When Felix saw her golden locks droop, he realized that his words had come out more harshly than he had intended. His countenance softened and compelled him to go to her.

"Oh, Darling. I'm sorry. I didn't mean it like that. You're always welcome here. I've just been so worried about you lately."

She smiled. "I know. It's ok."

He looked her up and down. "You know, sometimes I think more than just those medical lessons are rubbing off on you." Straightening back to his full height, he put his hands on his hips, shook his head, and sighed. "I just don't know what I'm going to do with the both of you."

"Well, I know what you can do," Master Marlow jumped in. "You can *be a good lad* and put all these clothes in the closet."

The butler conjured up the most contemptible glare he could. "Now don't you start."

While he busied himself thus, the master led the way to the library.

"What was that about?" Alvera asked.

He had to stifle a laugh. "Oh, nothing. Come on."

Once they had entered the cozy book-crammed room and settled into the spruce leather armchairs, they continued their initial conversation, asking each other what they had done to pass the time while they were sick and if they had any Christmas plans. Their confinement agendas were almost identical. They consisted mostly of reading and sleeping, but Alvera had also taken the time to snuggle with her cat. As for Christmas, both were planning on just spending it with family, a rather nerve-wracking yet exciting prospect for Master Marlow. He was about to tell Alvera about one of the books he had been reading, when Felix came sauntering into the room, his arms laden with a tray of tea and a couple of blankets, interrupting their visit yet again.

"I thought I'd bring you both some tea," he said, setting his load on one of the side tables and pouring the amber liquid into cups. He handed one to Alvera and the other to the master, who grudgingly accepted it. "I also brought some blankets. Here you go, Dear," he said, draping one across

Alvera's lap. "And here you go, Sir." The master's eyes flashed warningly, causing Felix to hesitate. Instead of covering him up, he simply folded the edges of the blanket back together and hung it over the back of his chair. "I'll just leave it there in case you need it." Patting him on the shoulder, the butler hurriedly shuffled out the door and headed back upstairs. "Let me know if you need anything else."

Alvera wrapped her slender hands tightly around her cup, pulled it closer to her, and let it rest on her lap. It was like a miniature heater insulating her entire body, and its steam bathed her face like the soothing warmth of a dog's tongue. She closed her eyes and allowed herself to sink deeper into the blanket and chair. Upon opening them again, she was met with the master's grumpy figure. She smiled at him. She understood his frustration, but Felix was only trying to be helpful. And she had to admit that she greatly appreciated his thoughtfulness.

When he finally noticed her loving look, the master's irritation melted away, and he went back to talking about his book. It was a compilation of inspirational poems that had been encouraging him during these trying times. He asked if she'd like to hear some, and she said yes. So, he began to read. However, after a little over half an hour had passed, he noticed her yawning over the top of his book. He lowered it and looked at her.

"Am I boring you?"

Alvera started in her seat. "What? Oh, no! No. I'm sorry. I'm just a little tired. That's all. Please, keep going."

"All right." He raised the book back to eye level. When he found his place, he opened his mouth as if to continue,

but no sound came out. He closed it and stared contemplatively at the pages ahead. Something was prompting him to
stop, and he knew what it was. This was the opportunity he
had been waiting for. Felix was upstairs, so he shouldn't be
able to hear. And everything seemed quiet enough. He listened for a moment. Yes, all was still. Now was his chance.
Without deviating his gaze, he slowly closed his book and
laid it in his lap.

"Alvera?" he softly spoke.

"Yes?"

"Can I tell you something?"

"Of course."

He paused for a moment, carefully choosing his words.
"This has been weighing heavily on my mind for quite
some time. I haven't shared it with anyone yet, but I need to
now. I know you can keep a secret, so I'm going to share it
with you. I ...I just want someone else to know." He paused
again. "I told you that I started feeling ill the day after I
invited my brothers over for dinner. Well, I don't think it
was a coincidence. When I was sick, I got to thinking—it
was one of the only things I could do at first—and I just
couldn't figure out how I had contracted pneumonia. It
wasn't like me to get sick, especially that sick. I didn't have
a compromised immune system, and I hadn't been around
anyone with the disease. It just didn't make any sense.

"So, I did some investigating, and what I found was
truly devastating. There was pneumococcus on my handkerchief, and one of my petri dishes of the bacteria was
missing. I still don't have any definite conclusions. I hope
it's not true, but ..."

He looked up at Alvera and found that she had fallen fast asleep, her head lolling slightly to one side. Her cup and saucer were slowly slipping from her limp hands. Before they could spill or crash to the floor, Master Marlow gently scooped them up and set them on the table next to her. He smiled at her peaceful figure, brushed her hair away from her face, and pulled the blanket back up from where it had fallen off her chest. Poor thing! She was exhausted. After all, she was still recovering. Perhaps it was best that she didn't know. At least, not yet. She had enough on her shoulders already without worrying about another one of the master's problems. The time would come, but for now, he would wait.

He yawned. Realizing that he was quite tired himself, he retired to his chair. However, no matter what position he situated himself in, he couldn't get comfortable. The leather was just too cool against his skin. Suddenly, he remembered the blanket Felix had left for him. He began to reach for it, but stubbornly turned away. No. He wasn't going to give in. But he was cold. And Alvera looked so cozy and content under her blanket. He couldn't take it. Relenting with an irritated sigh at his own weakness, Master Marlow grabbed the blanket and reclined beneath its embracing folds. It worked like warm milk, and before he knew it, he too had fallen asleep.

16

The next weekend, Alvera and Master Marlow went to his mother's house. He and his family had scheduled another day to visit with each other, and this time, he planned on staying overnight. Everyone was there except Andrew, who had been called into work that morning and wouldn't be back until late. Nevertheless, they still had a wonderful time even with just the four of them. Holiday specials and Christmas music created a soft ambience while they visited and played several games together, including cards, dominoes, and charades, the last being the highlight of the three. Mrs. Marlow was a rather clumsy ballerina. Alvera tried to imitate the wind but ended up looking more like a dancer than Mrs. Marlow had. Michael had to portray a family member and did a hilariously accurate depiction of Andrew, eliciting peals of laughter and a few reprimands from his mother. For the longest time, everyone thought that Master Marlow was either representing sternness or himself as he stood rigidly before them, but it turned out that he was actually trying to impersonate a tree.

After lunch, the master and Michael talked over quite

a few games of chess (almost all of which the master won, for his brother talked more than he strategized and simply wasn't very good at the game in general). However, no amount of losses could break his cheer or determination to keep trying. While they employed their time thus, Alvera helped Mrs. Marlow bake and decorate special Christmas biscuits and petit fours for family and friends. The festive aromas of vanilla, cinnamon, and sugar clouded the entire kitchen as they frosted the sweet treats with vibrant candy canes, stockings, bows, poinsettias, and stars. Once they were all complete, they put them in the refrigerator to cool and harden. They took the extras along with some hot tea to the men, who were very grateful for the refreshments.

That evening, they all gathered in the den and watched some Christmas movies that were on one of the seasonal marathons. Master Marlow was absolutely fascinated. The concept of television was all but foreign to him. After all, he had spent most of his life without it and other electricity-powered objects. Very few of the movies were familiar to him, but the ones that were took him back to his childhood. He felt as if he were reliving those fond winter memories while making new ones at the same time. He enjoyed every minute of it, but he especially enjoyed watching Alvera's expressions as she became caught up in the action and whimsy of the different films. It was as if he were watching a double feature.

Eventually, it grew late, and they all retired to bed except for Master Marlow. His mind was much too overstimulated to even think about sleep, for it still raced with the joy, excitement, and new experiences of the day. Perhaps the serenity of nature would calm its whirling gears. Sliding open one of the garden doors and closing it behind him, he stepped out into the frosty night. The air felt as if it were made of vaporized ice, causing the master's breath to rise in steamy puffs. He followed them up to the sky. It too was clouded over, for not a single star could penetrate its interwoven ethereal wisps. Perhaps it would snow. It was certainly cold enough. He lowered his gaze. The grass and trees that he knew lay in front of him were nothing but a black curtain, and not one sound, not even the wind, ruffled its midnight folds. All dreamed peacefully in a silent sleep.

Suddenly, the enchanting quiet was broken by a soft crunching of grass just around the corner of the front porch. It ceased as soon as the master jerked his head in its direction. He peered through the darkness, but he could barely even see a few feet in front of him.

"Who's there?" His question seemed to echo for miles, but no one answered. He cautiously moved closer to the source of the sound.

"What are you doing here?"

He froze. He knew that voice. The crunching steps began again, and slowly, Andrew emerged like a squid from his inky hideaway. Never once taking his eyes off him, he stalked in a semicircle away from his brother until he was directly opposite to him.

"I could ask you the same thing," Master Marlow retorted.

"No, that's not what I mean. What are you doing still alive?"

Andrew's question startled the master at first, but he

quickly realized that it confirmed what he had secretly known all along. "So, it was you," he whispered. He hadn't intended for his brother to hear him, but he did.

"Of course it was me. You're supposed to be the genius, Malchus. I thought you would have figured that out by now." He gave a haughty laugh. "I guess I really did get away with it right under everyone's noses, or rather, under your nose."

Master Marlow was silent for a moment before solemnly saying, "I just have one question." He paused. His brother waited for him to continue. "Why?"

All at once, Andrew's restrainedly calm demeanor burst open, revealing his suppressed anger. The master thought he could almost see his body quivering and his eyes glowing with rage through the dark. "Why? Why?! You of all people have the audacity to ask me why?!!" He tried reluctantly and rather unsuccessfully to control his voice. "Everything was perfect until you came along. You ruined our family legacy. From then on, we were shunned by the rest of our relatives as if our parents had committed some utterly immoral act to deserve such an ill-formed child. But no one ever *blamed you* for our misery and shame, even though you were the cause of it. Oh, no! If anything, they *pitied* you. It was always poor Malchus this and poor Malchus that. Poor Malchus indeed! Ha! You got all the attention, especially from Mother, and I bet you just loved it. After all, she always favored you. Don't think I didn't notice how she'd pull you onto her lap or hold you in her arms! I never got such special treatment! It was always about you! Because you were different!"

"Do you honestly think I wanted to be like this?" the master suddenly interrupted. "To be deformed? To be covered with scars?" He shook his head. "I never asked for any of this. And I certainly never wanted to be pitied. All I ever wanted was to be normal. You don't know how often I wished that I could be like you and Michael growing up. But no matter how many stars and dandelions I wished on, nothing ever changed. I didn't have a choice. I didn't have a say in the matter. This is simply how I was born, and the wolf did the rest. I ... I don't know what else to say. I'm sorry I can't change who I am."

Master Marlow lowered his head. He couldn't bear to look into his brother's hate-filled eyes any longer. As he pondered on all the pent-up emotions they had just released upon each other, he felt something cold and wet kiss the end of his crooked nose. It had begun to snow. Maybe the gentle flakes would have the same calming effect on Andrew as they did on him. However, they only seemed to irritate him even more like a swarm of flies, for his heated breaths grew louder like the snorting of an angry bull.

In between steamy puffs, he said, "No? Well, I can."

A fist aggressively collided with the master's left eye, knocking him backward. He squinted both eyes closed and clapped a hand over the injured one. Once all the little balls of light had vanished and the initial shock had worn off, he straightened and looked up at his brother. His arms were clenched, and his legs were bent in a wrestling stance.

"Fight back."

The words bounced off Master Marlow as if he were a

brick wall, for he did nothing. Andrew flashed his snarling teeth, lunged forward, and grabbed him by the collar.

"I SAID FIGHT BACK!!!"

He swung him around and flung him from his choking grip before jabbing at him again with his fists. The master did his best to avoid each bruising blow, a few of them coming so close that he could feel their wind spitting snowflakes in his face. All the while, he was slowly being backed into a corner. When his heels unexpectedly crashed into the brick border of the garden, he lost his balance and concentration. Seizing the opportunity to score another hit, Andrew punched his brother in the arm as hard as he could. It felt as if his knuckles had sunk through the skin all the way to the bone. With a grunt, the master fell to the ground.

"Come on, Malformed!" Andrew thundered, leering over his crumpled brother. "Mother's bragged so much about you being a fighter, so fight like the savage monster you are!" He kicked him in the side. Master Marlow winced and curled into an even tighter ball, but it wasn't the physical pain that hurt him the most.

Malformed. He remembered that loathsome name with a grimace. It was the name Andrew most often called him when they were boys. In fact, he had called him that in a situation very similar to the present one. The master found his younger self desperately plunging through a field of grass that towered far above his raven head. All he could hear were his own labored breaths and his brother's taunts pursuing him. Andrew had been trying to start a fight. Before things had gotten too out of hand, the master had bolted. Since then, however, he had learned that running away never solved anything; it only made things worse in the future. So, this time, he would not run, but just as he had not fought then, he also would not fight now.

Andrew swung his leg to goad the master with a second kick, but before the toe of his shoe could even graze his ribs, he rolled out of the way and scrambled back to his feet. His brother immediately came after him again with violent fists. Master Marlow continued to dodge, never once saying a word or engaging in the combat.

Suddenly, Andrew altered his attack and thrust both arms forward. Instinctively, the master blocked him with his own arms and found himself locked hand in hand with his brother. Their muscles quivered with the effort, Andrew's from trying to push Malchus over, and the master's from trying to keep himself upright. The snow melted and mixed with the drops of sweat collecting on their foreheads.

Through gritted teeth that seemed to hiss beneath his twitching mustache, Andrew spat, "You're pitiful! You always have been! Weak, disgusting, repulsive wretch! You never should have even been born!" He abruptly pulled away, causing Malchus to lurch forward. He quickly regained his footing. "You've disgraced the world with your hideous face! It will never accept you as one of its own because you're not!" He ran up to his brother and grabbed his shirt. "Show the world what you really are!"

Jerking with all his strength, he ripped the sooty cloth, revealing the master's twisted body. His pearly scars that were slashed across his chest and rippling up his arms shone in place of the stars. He felt just like a deer caught in the middle of a busy road, not knowing whether to flee or freeze. But there was nowhere to hide. He was completely exposed. Realizing this, Master Marlow resignedly hung his head and clutched his injured arm, which had begun to throb in the bitter cold. Andrew simply stared at the spectacle with superior satisfaction and a malicious sneer.

Inside, Alvera emerged from her room and softly pattered down the hall toward the kitchen to get a glass of water. When she came to the sliding glass doors, however, she paused. Her eyes lit up with excitement and wonder as she stared at the magical flurries floating down from the sky. She loved the snow. It was something she always wished for every year, but this time, it came with an unpleasant surprise.

She could just make out two dark figures lumbering back and forth through the fluttering flakes. Recognizing their silhouettes, she dashed back down the hall and began urgently knocking on Michael's bedroom door. "Mr. Michael! Mr. Michael!" He emerged bewildered.

"Yes? Oh! it's you, Alvera. What are you doing up? It's very late. You should be in bed."

"I know, but Mr. Marlow's in trouble!"

"What?"

"Hurry!"

Jogging, he followed Alvera to the doors, flipped on the flood lights, and stepped outside. He couldn't believe what he saw.

"Andrew!"

His brother immediately froze and turned his head as he was about to punch the master in the jaw. In the milky beams, he looked like a prisoner who had been caught beating up a fellow inmate. Michael began to march toward them.

"What in the world has gotten into you?"

Releasing the paralyzing grip he had on the master's shoulder, Andrew pulled his coat more tightly around himself and fled back around the porch into the obscuring darkness. Master Marlow backed away and protectively covered his naked torso with his cloak as Michael continued to approach. Seeing his brother's embarrassment and discomfort, he respectfully stopped.

"Malchus, are you all right?"

"Yes," he said in a husky voice, "I'm fine. Just get Alvera back in bed for me. I'll be in in a minute."

With a nod, Michael trudged back to the house and tried to usher Alvera out of the doorway. "Come on, Alvera. Everything's all right. Let's get you back into bed."

"Wait!" she cried, ducking under his arms and sprinting out the door. He turned and found her already halfway across the yard.

"Alvera!"

She kept running. When she was only a few feet from the master, however, she slowed her pace and walked the rest of the way to him. "Mr. Marlow," she panted as she tried to catch her breath, "are you sure you're all right?"

The master solemnly crossed the small gap between them, knelt down, reached a gnarled arm out of his cloak while making sure the rest of his mangled body was still covered, and placed a gentle hand on Alvera's shoulder. He looked into her crystal blue eyes that were anxiously scanning his face and smiled. "Alvera, don't worry about me. Right now, I'm more worried about you. You need to get inside out of this cold. Your body is still weak and could easily relapse back into illness." He straightened and pulled away.

"But …" Her protest ended with several coughs.

"Alvera!" Michael called again.

She looked at him before turning back to Master Marlow.

"Go on," he urged. "Michael will take good care of you."

She hesitated, her wide eyes and mouth seeming to say, "Yes, but what about you?"

He flashed another reassuring smile. "I'll be fine. I promise."

After gazing up at him a moment longer, Alvera reluctantly headed back toward the house. A relieved smile spread on Michael's face as he beckoned to her. "There we go. That's it. Come on in." Closing the door behind her, he placed an arm around her shoulders and led her down the hall. His arm flinched almost as soon as it touched her. "Oh! Alvera, you're freezing! Come on. Let's get you warm." All the way to her room, Alvera kept glancing back over her shoulder to see if Master Marlow got in all right. But she never saw him. Not even the hem of his cloak.

* * *

"There," Michael said stepping back. "Is that better?"

Upon getting Alvera into bed, he had grabbed some more pillows for her to be able to lie in a more upright position, layered several extra blankets on top of the sheets that were already there, pulled them all up, and tucked them snugly around her shoulders.

Without looking up, she nodded. Michael grew concerned and monitored her every movement more closely than before. Was she sick? Had she stayed outside too long? Had he not gotten her in quick enough? Slowly, her gaze drifted toward the window, and he understood.

"You're worried about him. Aren't you?"

She finally looked at him and nodded again.

"Don't be. Malchus is a strong individual. Very strong. He'll be fine. I'm sure of it. Trust me. He's been through much worse than this."

Yes. She knew that. Silence crept over the room as they both fell into deep contemplation. It was only broken once by a few stifled coughs from Alvera, but it was enough to wake Michael from his reverie and give him an idea that might help lighten the mood.

Sitting at the foot of the bed, he looked at the ailing girl and smiled. "You know what our mother used to do whenever any of us were feeling a little under the weather?"

"What?"

"She'd read to us. In fact … hold on a second." He excitedly sprang from the bed and dashed out the door. Alvera just stared after him with confused curiosity. When he returned, he clutched a book in his hands. He sat back down on the bed and showed it to her. "Have you ever read *Great Expectations* by Charles Dickens?"

She nodded.

"It's a wonderful story. Isn't it? It was always one of my favorites as a boy, and it still is today. In fact, I was in the middle of reading it when you knocked on my door." He looked wistfully at the front cover and ran his fingers over its worn hardback surface. "I know you're not a little girl anymore, but … would you mind if I read it to you?"

She shook her head as a slight smile tugged at the corners of her mouth. He noticed it and positively glowed with joy from his golden curls to his rosy cheeks. "All right then." Rising to his feet, he made his way to a cushioned armchair in a corner of the room facing the bed, sat down, and began to read. He had only made it to chapter three when his eyelids began to grow heavy. In a matter of seconds, he succumbed to their lazy tug and dozed off. Alvera, however, still sat wide awake in bed. She couldn't sleep. She just couldn't.

Slipping out from underneath the covers, she cautiously tiptoed out the door and down the hall. Once again, she stopped in front of the glass doors, but this time, she sat down. It was still snowing. The feathery flakes fell in great waves like powdered sugar from the sky, thickening the white carpet that had been rolled out over the ground. It was completely unblemished, spotless, and pure, and it seemed to illuminate the surrounding landscape with an ethereal glow, even though the moon and stars remained hidden. But it was only a façade. Its beauty was tarnished. Its innocence tainted. Just like Alvera, it too had witnessed and been affected by that horrific event. Tears began to stream from her eyes. Closing them, she folded her hands, lifted them to her chest, and began to pray.

17

Master Marlow stared at the side door and debated whether or not to open it. It was the next morning. He had already dropped Alvera off at her house and was now back at his own. He peeked through the screen. Felix was at the counter scrambling some eggs. Stepping back, he looked at his reflection in the glass. He frowned. Nope. It was much too obvious. He couldn't go in like that. He pulled up his hood and looked again. It wasn't much better. In fact, it would only make the butler even more suspicious. Perhaps if he were fast…No. He sighed. He didn't have a choice. He would just have to try and hope it worked. Keeping his head down, he grabbed the handle and ducked through the door.

Felix immediately greeted him. "Ah! good morning, Sir."

"Good morning," he mumbled as he took huge, hurried strides across the floor.

"How was your visit?"

"Fine. Fine."

"Just 'fine'? Wait a minute."

The master caught the newel post and froze just as he was about to bound up the stairs. Turning his head ever so slightly, he looked out the corner of his right eye. Felix was now facing his direction and, to the master's horror, was staring right at him. He gave a nearly inaudible groan. He had almost made it. Almost! The butler drew closer.

"Where are you going in such a hurry?"

He quickly thought up a plausible explanation. "I was just going upstairs to put my things away and freshen up. I'll be right back down."

The butler wasn't convinced. He continued to meticulously scan the master up and down until his eyes came to rest on his hood. "What are you doing with your hood pulled up? I thought you were trying not to wear it as much."

"It's cold outside. Isn't it?"

"Well, you're inside now. Why don't you take it off?"

"I…I can't. My hands are full." He lifted up the small travel bag packed with toiletries and clothes that he had taken to his mother's house as proof. It was by far his weakest excuse. He feared that he had destroyed his delicate ruse, but to his surprise, Felix believed him, as evidenced by his considerably brightened countenance.

He shook his head and chuckled. "Oh, Sir. When will you ever learn to ask for help? I say. Your stubbornness never ceases to amaze me. Here. I'll get it for you."

"No!" the master panicked, shrinking away from the butler's hand. His smile drooped. Noticing this, the master instantly tried to rebuild his calm demeanor. "I mean…No, that's all right, Felix. I'll get it once I get up to my room."

"I don't mind, Sir. Really. It's not a problem." He reached for the black fabric again, and Master Marlow backed away again.

"No."

"I can get it."

"I said no!"

"Why? Are you hiding something?"

"No!"

"Then, just let me get it!"

The two continued in this manner until Felix had chased Master Marlow nearly halfway across the room. When he backed into one of the chairs in the den, the butler seized his chance and threw back the master's hood. He gasped and covered his mouth at what he saw. A splotchy purple and black bruise completely surrounded the master's left eye and spread part of the way down his cheek. His eyelid and surrounding skin were slightly swollen, and his eye itself looked as if it had been framed in blood.

"Sir! What happened?!"

He sighed and turned away. "It's nothing."

"It is not! You've been beat up!"

Giving an irritated grunt, he pushed past the distressed butler and headed toward the stairs.

"Did Andrew do this?"

No response.

"Did he?"

"So what if he did?" the master suddenly snapped.

Felix was silent for a moment before uttering a sound that was somewhere between a moan and a sigh. "This is exactly what I was afraid of," he said, propping an elbow in one hand and resting the other hand against his cheek. "I just knew something like this would happen one of these days." He shook his head. "I'm sorry, Sir, but this is for your own good. I cannot allow you to go back to your mother's house anymore."

Halfway up the stairs, Master Marlow abruptly stopped. "Excuse me?"

Believing that the master had not heard him clearly, he repeated himself. "I can't allow you to go back. It's far too dangerous."

The master slowly turned to face him. "You can't *allow* me?"

"That's right."

"Who gave *you* authority over *me*?"

Taken aback by the incensed question, Felix realized that he may have overstepped his boundaries. "Well…uh…no one, Sir. I…I didn't mean it like that. I was really just saying it out of concern for you. As a friend to a friend…or as a father to a child."

"I'm not a child, Felix!" he bellowed. "And you can't control me!" He turned back around and continued marching up the stairs.

"I know, Sir, but I'm trying to protect you. It seems as if your brother is out to kill you!" (He didn't realize how accurate he was being.) "I mean, every time you're around him, something happens."

"I can take care of myself."

"I just don't want to see you get hurt again."

Master Marlow paused at the top of the stairs and sighed. He knew Felix meant well, but he didn't understand. He couldn't. "Felix," he solemnly began without fully turning his head, "people get hurt every day. It's a part of life. I spent twenty years trying to keep myself from it. If I couldn't do it, you can't either." After waiting for just a moment longer, the master stepped into the hall and disappeared from sight.

<h1 style="text-align:center">18</h1>

"It's not as bad as it looks," the master said, removing a cold compress from his bludgeoned eye. He sat at his desk in the study. Alvera, who had come over to check on him later that same day, sat facing him. She looked at his ghastly injury for a moment before lowering her gaze to her lap. Master Marlow followed it and noticed her hands fidgeting uneasily with her fingers. He looked back at what he could see of her face. "What is it?"

At first, the uncomfortable silence surrounding her was his only answer, but after a few seconds of contemplation, her tiny voice whispered, "I just don't understand." She paused and looked up at him. "Why would he do this to you?"

"Because he tried to kill me."

Her eyes widened, and her forehead creased with confusion. The master proceeded to explain.

"I've been wanting to tell you for quite some time, but an opportunity never presented itself until now. My illness was no accident. I did some investigating and found pneumococcus on the handkerchief that Andrew gave me when I invited him and Michael over for dinner. That night, he had shown great interest in the incubator, and sure enough, when I checked it, one of my specimens of the bacteria was gone. He probably didn't know what he was grabbing; he just hoped it would be something lethal. I didn't want to believe it at first, but after last night…" He broke off with a sigh, closed his eyes, and shook his head. "There really is no denying it. And it all stems from past bitterness, hatred, and jealousy."

"If you've known this all along, why haven't you called the police?"

He sighed again. "I have thought about it, but I have no solid evidence. All of it has either been thrown away or tampered with. It would be my word against his. Besides…I really don't want to turn him in. After all, he is my brother, and I've worked too hard to grow closer to him just to drive us further apart. I don't want to lose him altogether."

Alvera nodded. She understood.

Silence encased the room as the two friends became absorbed with their own thoughts. It was so quiet that Alvera wondered if the master could hear what she was thinking. Her mind's voice seemed to boom as loudly as if it were being projected through a megaphone into the soundless void. Master Marlow looked back up at her as if he had heard it. "Felix thinks I shouldn't go over to my mother's house anymore. What do you think?"

She pondered for a moment. "Well, you can't stop seeing your family. Not after you've become so close. But I do have to agree a little bit with Mr. Felix. I think it would be best if you didn't go when you know Andrew will be there."

He mulled over what she had said and nodded. "I figured you'd say something like that, but both of you are probably right. I want to keep reaching out to my brother, but every time I try, it turns into a confrontation." He sighed. "I just don't know what else I can do."

"You can always pray for him."

"I know. I have been."

"Well, I do know something else you could try."

"What?"

"Writing to him like you do with me."

The master suddenly felt as if somebody had slapped a dunce hat onto his head. Of course! It was the perfect solution. Why hadn't he thought of it before?

Alvera continued, "I do the same thing with my uncle because … well … he and my father don't exactly get along either."

He looked into her eyes, his own round with wonder. He had no idea that she had been struggling with a similar situation. They had much more in common than the master could have ever imagined, and more than ever, he was glad that he had someone like Alvera in his life who truly understood him. He listened more intently as she elaborated further.

"They were really close, and we used to get together all the time. But then they had an argument. I was younger when it happened, so I still don't understand what it was about. Since then, though, I've started writing to him every day in the hopes that something will soften his heart. Sometimes I even send him pictures or little gifts."

"Has he ever responded?" he asked hopefully.

"No," she said, her cheerfulness fading momentarily, "but that doesn't matter. Whether they answer or not, the letters show them that you still care and are thinking about them."

She was right. As with all his other efforts, he couldn't expect immediate results. Family issues took time to untangle, and in his brother's case, an extensive amount of time. He would just have to continue to be patient. Who knew? Perhaps Andrew would see these letters as a less volatile approach at friendliness. And maybe they would even be the thrust he needed to change.

"Ok. I'll give it a try."

* * *

Dear Andrew,

I hope you're doing well. I know we haven't been able to see each other very much, mainly because of our work schedules, so I thought I'd keep in touch by writing to you. Alvera and I do the same thing. I know it's a bit old fashioned, but I thought it would be a fun way for the two of us to get to know each other again.

Did you see the snow we got last night at mother's? It was absolutely beautiful! I think we got just as much, if not more, here. I love how quiet it makes everything. It's as if the whole world just stops and stares in awe at its brilliance. Alvera came over and built a snowman in the front yard. She made him look just like the snowman from that old cartoon we used to watch when we were kids. I remember we used to act it out. You would pretend to be the magician, Michael always wanted to be the rabbit, and I would play the snowman.

Our horses, Obsidian and Frank, have been enjoying the snow too. Well, Obsidian has. He's been running around and rolling in it just like an overgrown dog. He'll even chase snowballs if you throw one for him. I've never seen a horse act so. As for Frank, let's just say he'll be happy when spring gets here. Poor fellow! He looks absolutely miserable. He just stands there in his stall with the deepest of scowls on his face. I think he may have arthritis in his joints, for when I checked his legs the other day, they were exceedingly stiff. I'm going to go to the village pet store and see if I can find some medicine that will make him more comfortable.

On a lighter note, can you believe that Christmas is only a few weeks away? Felix nearly started bouncing off the walls with excitement when I told him that he could decorate the house. It's the first time he's ever gotten to do it because I never would let him before. You see, ever since I left home, Christmas lost its joy for me. Instead of a time of love and celebrating the birth of our Savior with family and friends, it became a bitter reminder of what I had lost. But now that I have my family back, I can honestly say that I too am starting to feel excited again about Christmas.

I guess it's a combination of a lot of things that I haven't done in a long time. Picking out a tree. Decorating it. Baking. Now, I am by no means a chef, but I promised Felix that I would help him make fruitcake. He's always wanted to make a traditional Christmas dish. I'm not too optimistic about it, but it was a better option than figgy pudding. I'm also going to get to spend Christmas with Alvera and her family for the first time. I can't wait to share in their traditions and see the look on Alvera's face when she opens my gift to her. She wants to go into the medical field, so I'm giving her her own stethoscope. If you should see her, don't tell her. This is our little secret. But most of all, I'm looking forward to spending Christmas with my own family again. I hope you are too.

Love,
your brother Malchus

This was the first of many similar letters Master Marlow wrote to his brother. He never once answered any of them, but just as Alvera had encouraged, the master persevered. Day after day, he faithfully wrote to him, sending occasional pictures and gifts as well. Something had to give, and it wasn't going to be him. He was determined to fight for his brother, even though Andrew would have him fight against him. He wanted his brother back. He had to get him back. He just had to.

Well, Christmas came and went, and it was even more wonderful than the master ever remembered it being. On Christmas Eve, he and Felix spent the entire day with Alvera and her family. They made biscuits just like they had done at his mother's house, but they also made a birthday cake. When Master Marlow asked who it was for, they explained that it was one of their family traditions. Every year, they would bake a cake to celebrate the birth of Jesus, and on December 25, they would light a candle, sing, and blow it out just like they would at any other birthday party. This year, since it was Master Marlow and Felix's first time spending Christmas with the Levlen family, they got the honor of decorating the cake. The master piped out the words in his most elegant cursive, while Felix squirted dainty red and green puffs around the edges and dusted the top with an assortment of sprinkles. By the time they were done, the cake looked good enough to be displayed in the window of a bakery. Anita said that they would definitely have to share such an exquisite work of art with the rest of their family and friends.

That evening, they planned on going to a candlelight service at their church, but before they went, Master Marlow wanted to give Alvera her gift. Immediately after opening it, she rushed over to him and gave him a hug. She had been wanting a stethoscope for a long time, but it was even more special because it had come from the master himself. Felix also had something for her. It was a collection of some of the greatest literary works in history. She loved it just as much as the stethoscope. Her gifts to them were homemade. For Felix, she made a potholder since she knew how much he liked to cook. Its quilt-like fabric was covered with various breeds of horses, two of which closely resembled Obsidian and Frank. Tears of joy brimmed up in his eyes when he saw it.

As for the master, his gift appeared to be no more than

a rather plain-looking folder, but when he opened it, he found an explosion of colors and life. It was a scrapbook full of various photos that had been taken over the course of their friendship. It had everything from the very first picture of the three of them standing together in the grass to a picture of Alvera holding her beloved cat. Master Marlow could feel his turbulent emotions trying to overpower him as he relived each precious memory. The time and the care that she had taken to make something just for him. It was the most thoughtful gift he could have ever received. There was just one thing missing. On the front of the scrapbook, one rectangular frame had been left empty. Alvera explained that she had saved that space for today. Motioning for him to follow her, they joined Felix and the rest of the family around the tree and posed for a picture. As soon as it had printed from the camera, the master slipped it into its designated spot and smiled at it.

After that, they headed to the church. Wreaths hung on every door, garland was strung in every window, and welcoming smiles glowed on everyone's faces. It was the pure warmth and joy of the Spirit, and the master could feel it flowing and filling up the hearts of the congregation, including his own, throughout the entire service. But the most glorious part happened at the very end. After the pastor had said the closing prayer, everyone rose from their seats and formed a circle that encompassed the entire sanctuary. Candles were then passed around. Once everyone had one, two of them were lit on either side of the circle.

Leaning their flickering candles toward their neighbors', these first flame-bearers began spreading the light. Then the next person, and the next, and the next, until the entire congregation had been transformed into a living ring of fire. The pianist struck a note, and they all started singing, "Silent Night," acapella. Most people softly sang the melody. Some came in on various harmonies, and a few belted out notes that were rather off key and off rhythm as loud as they could. But that didn't matter. Soon, the music swelled and blended together until the church seemed to ring with the voices of thousands of angels. The people themselves even began to resemble ruddy-faced cherubim in the heavenly glow of the candles. Overall, it was the most beautiful display the master had ever experienced.

On the way back to the Levlen household, they took a few detours to look at Christmas lights. Some houses were modestly decorated with a single strand of white icicles outlining the roof and perhaps a couple of reindeer standing in the yard, while others dazzled the eyes with a kaleidoscope of colors. The master had no idea that electric lights could be so beautiful. In fact, there was almost something magical about them. But it was even more magical to watch Alvera's expressions as she eagerly gazed out the car windows, her face lighting up just as brightly as each twinkling house they passed. It was a wonderful way to wrap up Christmas Eve.

Christmas Day, however, was another story. Master Marlow had hoped that the excitement and joy that had built up in his heart the day before would stay with him. It did, to some extent, but as soon as he climbed out of bed that morning, he felt the familiar cloak of depression gently drape itself around his shoulders. The pain. The loneliness. They were still there, and he suddenly realized that it might take several Christmases before they completely went away, if they ever did. There was also still separation between him and his family. He knew why it had to be this way, at least for the time being, but it didn't make it any easier for him. Right now, the closest thing he had to a family Christmas was the scrapbook Alvera had made, so grabbing it from beside his bed, he took it downstairs with him.

Everything was dark except for the Christmas tree, which Felix had left plugged in all night. Turning on a lamp, the master sat down in one of the chairs in the den and began flipping through the treasured book. He thought it would make him feel better, but if anything, it only made him feel worse. All these happy faces…together. And here he was, more miserable and alone than ever. If only this could be his reality. Right here. Right now. It was right there. He could touch it, but he feared that he could never fully grasp it because he never had been able to before.

As he silently cried over the book filled with so many seemingly broken dreams, Felix came down the stairs. Master Marlow heard him and quickly wiped away his tears as best he could.

"Happy Christmas, Sir!" Felix greeted, rounding the master's chair.

"Happy Christmas, Felix."

"What are you looking at? Oh! it's the little scrapbook Alvera made for you." He leaned over the master's shoulder and began pointing at different pictures. "I remember that. That was when you and Alvera went horseback riding together."

"Yes."

"And this one with the frog. It came in one of her letters. Didn't it?"

"Yes." His voice was growing softer and more tremulous by the second.

"Aww! And look at that one. What a good picture of Alvera and her family."

He said the word. The master's whole body began to quiver as he redoubled his efforts to hold back the tears that were already pooling up in his eyes again. His vision blurred. He couldn't speak. Instead, he simply nodded, but the movement unwittingly shook one of his sorrowful drops loose. It landed with a soft splat against one of the laminated pages. He discreetly tried to wipe it off, but it was too late. Felix had already seen it. He craned his neck to catch a glimpse of the master's face, but he instinctively turned away and tucked his chin closer to his chest.

"Sir, are you all right?"

He nodded again, and another drop fell onto the opposite page. Closing the book, he set it to the side, for the rest of his tears were now falling in rapid succession. Embarrassed, he furiously began wiping his face. He never wanted anyone to see him like this, but Felix had caught him in his vulnerability, and there was nothing he could do about it.

The butler suddenly realized his mistake and was also moved to tears. "Oh, Sir! I … I'm so sorry! I forgot!"

His empathetic cries turned to bawling sobs just as the master managed to get his own grief under control.

Realizing that they both needed to be comforted, he rose from his chair and embraced the sniffling butler. Neither spoke as they stood there clutching each other as if their very lives depended on it. Felix simply couldn't, and Master Marlow didn't in order to respectfully let his friend spend his sorrow in silence.

After several minutes, Felix finally calmed down and pulled away. He held the master by the shoulders and looked him directly in the eye. "Sir," he shakily began, tears still streaming down his face, "I know this time of year has always been difficult for you. And I know it's even more difficult under the present circumstances. But it's going to be all right. It's going to be a great day." He slapped one of the master's shoulders and smiled. "Now, come on! Let's make this the best Christmas we've ever had!"

To the master's surprise, it did turn out to be the most wonderful Christmas ever, even though it started out quite gloomy. It was all thanks to Felix and his contagious optimism. He knew exactly what to do to make everything better, and the master was reminded, yet again, of just how thankful he was to have such a kind and compassionate friend.

Their day was filled with dozens of fun activities (all planned by Felix, of course) from exchanging gifts to taking an exhilarating ride on their horses through the snow. But the highlight of them all was baking the fruitcake. Just as the master had expected, it was an absolute disaster. Oh, the cake looked all right. In fact, it was perfect. The dough was tanned to a rich gingerbread brown. An assortment of nuts and dried yellow, red, and green fruits textured its surface, and the whole thing seemed to glisten with a sugary glaze. There was just one problem. It was completely inedible. That cake was as hard and heavy as a handful of bricks. The only things you could use it for were as a doorstop or perhaps as a secret weapon to knock someone out. However, it was good for one other thing: laughter. When Felix plopped that fruitcake fiasco on the counter, Master Marlow laughed so hard that he doubled over and had to lean on the table for support. Soon, Felix was laughing right along with him. He was just glad to see his friend happy and enjoying himself once again.

The next day, since Andrew had to go back to work, the master finally got to spend Christmas with his family. It wasn't the same as getting together with them on Christmas Day, but they still had a wonderful time, nonetheless. Still, he hoped for change. Maybe by next year, things would be different.

19

Before Master Marlow knew it, January had arrived, and he found himself walking through a snow-covered park while tossing a snowball back and forth with his brother, Michael. He laughed as the ball shattered in the master's hands.

"Your turn again."

They were playing a game. Whoever missed the ball or had it crumble in his hands had to tell an interesting fact about himself. So far, they had all burst on the master. He gave an irritated grunt as he brushed the clumps of snow from his gloves and coat.

"Why do these things keep busting on me?"

"Because, apparently, you can't catch."

"No, I think it's because *someone* doesn't pack the snow-balls very well."

"Oh, come on, Malchus. Just go."

He sighed. "All right. Let's see. Well, aside from being a doctor, I like to read, write, and sew."

"Sewing? Really? Wow! I never would've guessed that. Did Mother teach you? You know she likes to crochet."

"No, I actually taught myself, and with the help of some books I learned how to make my own clothes."

"Really?"

He nodded.

"So, did you make all this?" he asked, indicating the master's outfit.

"Yes. Well, except for the scarf, coat, and gloves, of course."

"Wow! That's impressive!"

They began tossing another snowball around. This time, it shattered on Michael. He laughed again. "You finally got me! Now, let me think. What's something interesting about me? Oh! I've got a good one! In high school, I dressed up as a ballerina."

The master turned and gave his brother a funny look. "Do I even want to know the story behind this?"

"Oh yes, you do. Trust me."

They approached a bench at the top of a hill that overlooked the town. After sweeping off the cushion of snow that had collected in its seat, they sat down, and Michael continued his story.

"When I got to high school, I wanted to be one of the popular kids. You know…just to fit in for once. Now, I wasn't athletic by any means. I never had been, but no one was more popular than the school athletes, so I decided to try out for football. I tried out every year, and every year, I never made the cut. To make matters worse, the football team always teased me about my repeated failures. I never could run into them without being the punch line of one of their jokes. Instead of rising to the glorious heights of popularity, I had sunk to the most degrading levels of humiliation. However, during my senior year, it looked as if my social status had hopes of being reversed.

"After failing yet another tryout, the football team approached me. I thought they were just going to poke fun like they always did, but instead, they offered me a deal. They said they'd put in a good word for me with the coach if I did this one thing. Tomorrow, they were all going to come to school dressed up as ballerinas for the initiation of the new members. If I joined them, they said that they could almost guarantee a position for me on the team. At that point, I was willing to do almost anything to be in their group, so of course, I agreed.

"So, the next morning, I came waltzing into school in the leotard, tutu, tights, and slippers they had given me. I didn't care how ridiculous I looked. I was too absorbed in the exciting reality of finally becoming a football player. However, when the rest of the team met me in the hall, I realized that the whole thing had been nothing more than a cruel trick. Not one of them was wearing the dance attire, and they just stood there and laughed me to shame. It was the worst prank they had ever played on me. I wanted to disappear or, somehow, melt into the background, but there was no way that was going to happen. Since I had so naively trusted the others to keep their end of the deal, I didn't bother to bring a change of clothes with me. I was stuck in that bubble-gum nightmare suit for the rest of the day, and it eventually sent me to the principal's office for dressing inappropriately." He chuckled. "Yes, it was terrible, but not as terrible as what could have happened."

"What?"

"I could have ended up with the wrong kinds of friends."

The master smiled at his brother's astute observation. Michael always seemed to find a positive outcome even in the most trying of circumstances. For that reason, he often reminded him of Felix and Alvera. They had no idea how much of an encouragement they were to him. He needed more people like that in his life.

"Well, speaking of friends, look who it is," Michael suddenly exclaimed, leaning forward on the edge of his seat.

The master followed his intense gaze toward the town resting at the bottom of the hill and spotted Andrew sitting with arms and legs crossed at a table outside a small café. He kept anxiously looking around and shaking his feet as if he were waiting for someone.

"That little fibber," his brother continued as they both watched. "He told me he was too busy to spend time with us today. Busy indeed. Hmph! What does he think he's doing down there?"

Andrew abruptly stood up as a woman with bouncy chestnut curls approached his table. He pulled out the chair opposite to his for her to sit down. Once they were both seated, they began talking.

"Ah, it's Brenda," Michael said, his curiosity satisfied.

"Brenda?"

"Oh! that's right. You never got her name. That's Andrew's fiancé."

Aha! So that was the mystery girl.

"Now, as far as Andrew knows, none of us have ever

seen Brenda, and that's all the knowledge we need to take with us when we leave this park. Got it?"

The master nodded. "Wait," he added, scrunching up his brows. "How did you know what she looks like?"

"Oh, I've seen her dozens of times."

"How?"

His brother hesitated before mumbling, "By spying on them."

"Michael."

"What? All siblings do it when it comes to relationships."

Master Marlow simply smiled and shook his head as he directed his attention back toward the couple. He wondered why Andrew was so determined to keep Brenda hidden as much as possible from the rest of his family. As far as he could tell, she seemed to be an agreeable, polite, and quite beautiful lady. One that any mother would be proud to call her daughter-in-law. There was no fear of her being rejected, so what else did he have to be afraid of? Just then, Brenda turned, giving the master a clearer view of her face, and he began to understand what all the secrecy might be about.

"Why is she wearing a medical mask?"

"I don't know," Michael said, absentmindedly picking at a hangnail. "But almost every time they go into town together, she has one on, even when it's hot outside. I'm thinking she might be a germaphobe or something." The master didn't think so, but he didn't say anything. "Regardless, if Andrew knew what all I knew, he'd kill me."

"No," the master interjected, "he would rather kill me over you."

"Oh, don't say things like that!" his brother countered, playfully slapping him on the knee.

They both fell silent as their gazes slowly drifted over the magical winter landscape. The master looked past Andrew and the dozens of other pedestrians trudging through the slushy streets to the distant snow-covered rooftops of the town. They reminded him of the miniature animatronic Christmas villages that were still being displayed in various storefront windows. Just like those whirring and twinkling models, this real-life version could have captivated him for hours, but with Michael around, he knew that he wouldn't get that luxury. Sure enough, the blissful tranquility only lasted a few minutes before it was disrupted again.

"How are things between you and Andrew, anyway?"

"I don't know. I mean…I haven't seen him since that night. It's just too dangerous for me to meet him in person anymore, but I have been writing him letters to keep in touch."

His brother nodded and mused aloud to himself, "That would explain the scraps of paper I've been finding in the fireplace."

Master Marlow looked at his brother as if he had just stabbed him in the heart with an icicle. "He's been burning them?"

Michael suddenly realized that his brother had overheard him and laid a hand on his shoulder to comfort him. "Oh, Malchus, I'm so sorry."

Shrugging him off, the master hunched over, shook his drooping head, and sighed. "I give up."

"What?" Michael exclaimed, his pale eyes wide with alarm. "No! You can't give up!"

"Why not?"

"Because…that's not who you are. You're not a quitter. You're a fighter. I've seen that throughout my entire life." The master had never heard his brother speak so passionately before. "You didn't limit yourself because of your physical deformities. You were determined to show others that you were just as capable as they were, and no matter how big or how small, you never let any obstacle stop you from pursuing your dreams." He paused. "I never told you this, but…I've always looked up to you more than I ever looked up to Andrew."

For the first time since he had begun sulking, Master Marlow met his brother's earnest gaze. His own eyes sparkled with incredulity. Him? He had always looked up to…him?

Sensing the master's disbelief, Michael flashed an encouraging smile and continued, his voice growing thick with emotion. "You're such an inspiration to me, Malchus. You're brilliant, successful, and so, so strong. Things that I only wish I could be. I'm not smart. After all, I flunked out of college my very first semester. I'm not successful. If I were, maybe I'd be able to keep the same job for more than a year. And I'm certainly not strong, at least, not strong enough to stand on my own. I mean…I'm a forty-three-year-old man who still lives at home with his mother. How pathetic can you get? I'm sure people look down on me. Think I'm a failure. A burden. Useless."

He stopped. The master recognized the dejection on his

brother's downcast face. It was a look he was painfully familiar with. The look of a man who was tortured daily by the malignant lies he had allowed to take root in his heart. He gently spoke his brother's name, but before he could even begin to console him, Michael sprang back with a new burst of optimism.

"But people used to think the same things about you, and look at you now! Look at all that you've accomplished! You proved everyone wrong, and that's why I admire you so much. You give me the courage to keep trying and the hope that one day, I'll be able to conquer my obstacles as well. Because if you could do it, surely, I can too."

"Michael," the master said, his heart on the verge of breaking, "I appreciate your words of encouragement, but…I don't deserve such high praise."

"Don't be so modest. You've been put down far too much in your life. It's time someone started lifting you up."

"No, it's not. You shouldn't think so highly of me."

"Why not? Look at your life."

"I have, and it's nothing I would ever want anyone to imitate."

"How can you say such a thing? You're an inspiration."

"Then you don't know me very well at all," the master blurted rather harshly, stunning his brother into silence. "I didn't always persevere or overcome my hardships like you would believe me to have done. It's no coincidence that I disappeared after that horrendous article was published about me. My colleagues had framed me for something I hadn't done, all because they wanted my position. That was the last straw for me. I was tired of being bullied. Tired of being judged by my appearance, and tired of struggling to achieve my dreams just to have someone else steal them away from me. So, I left, and for the next twenty years, I hid from the world that I had come to hate. I gave up. So, no. I am nothing to be admired."

An awkward tension filled the air as the two brothers stared intensely at one another. Michael couldn't believe what he had just heard, and Master Marlow suddenly couldn't believe what he had just said. Coloring with embarrassment, he slowly turned away. He had only ever told that story in its entirety to Alvera. He had never planned on sharing it with anyone else, but there it was. Out in the open. And he couldn't take it back. He closed his eyes. He just knew that Michael would never view him the same way again.

A gentle pressure draped itself around his shoulders. The master looked up and saw that Michael had scooted closer and had wrapped his arm around him. His curious gaze wandered onto his brother's face. Fresh tears glistened like perfectly shaped drops of sleet in the corners of his eyes as he smiled sympathetically. He was smiling! His brother was smiling at him! And that mindboggling grin only widened as he tenderly said, "But you came back."

His statement only caused the master to blush and lower his head again. "Only because of Alvera. If it weren't for her, I'd still be hidden away."

"That's all right. We can't always overcome our difficulties on our own. Sometimes we need a little help. The important thing is that we keep going, and you have. So, according to my definition, that means you still haven't given up." They looked at each other again before Michael continued. "So, please…don't give up on Andrew. He needs you."

Michael was right. He needed to keep trying. It was the right thing to do. He just needed to keep his focus on what he was fighting for: not what his brother was at the moment, but what he could be in the future. After thinking all of this over, the master nodded in agreement.

Overflowing with joy, his brother gave him a firm hug before leaning back and dabbing at his runny eyes and nose with his scarf. He gave an exaggerated sigh. "Well, enough of this depressing talk." Standing up, he jogged around behind the bench.

Master Marlow, however, remained seated. He was far too pensive to even have the slightest interest in what his brother was doing. Then, he heard his name.

"Hey, Malchus!"

He looked behind him just in time to catch a snowball with his face. Michael nearly fell backwards with laughter into the snow.

"I can't believe you fell for that!"

"Well, I wasn't exactly expecting it," he fumed, wiping the rest of the freezing mush from his eyes.

"You weren't supposed to! It's a snowball fight! And it's about time I had a proper one with my brother. Now come on!"

The master glared at his brother for a moment before turning back around. "No."

"Oh, come on, Malchus!"

"Not right now. I'm not in the mood."

A snowball shattered defiantly against the back of his head. He turned, and another one splattered all over his face again. Soon, he was being pelted with a barrage of snowballs. At first, his reprimands to his brother were stern, but very quickly, they lost all seriousness and were even interspersed with laughter as the master futilely attempted to block the oncoming attack.

"Hey! Help! Michael! Stop!"

"I won't stop unless you join me!"

"All right! All right! You're asking for it!" he said finally rising from the bench. "But if you get frostbite, don't come running to me!"

With that, the ultimate snowball battle began, and Michael quickly realized that the master was the stronger opponent. Nevertheless, they both had fun giggling, chasing, and tackling each other like a couple of overgrown schoolboys all over the snowy hilltop. It was the most fun they had ever had together.

20

Dear Andrew,

How have you been? I can't believe the new year is already here. I hope it's been good for you so far. It's gotten off to a better start than I expected, thanks to a walk in the park with Michael the other day. I'm sure he's told you all about it. Hardly anyone had been there since the most recent snow. Everything was so smooth and pristine. It was absolutely breathtaking. I wish I had taken a picture for you to see.

Aside from sightseeing, we talked and wandered around for what seemed like hours on the various trails, and to finish off, we had our very first snowball fight together. It was so much fun. I wish you could've been there.

Master Marlow paused and reread what he had just written. *I wish you could've been there.* Did he really mean that? Yes, he supposed he did. He dipped his quill in the inkpot and lowered it back to the paper, but it didn't touch it this time. It just hovered indecisively in the air. His mind had drawn a blank. Ever since he learned that Andrew had been burning the letters he had been sending him, he found it increasingly difficult to write more of them. He just didn't know what to say anymore.

With a sigh, he dunked his quill back in the inkpot, laid the letter next to it, rubbed his weary eyes, leaned back, and yawned. It was late. He needed to get some sleep. He would just have to finish his letter tomorrow. After all, he wouldn't be sending it until then anyway.

Just then, there was a frantic knocking at the front door. Master Marlow banged his head against the back of his chair. Felix was already in bed. He would have to get it himself. Reluctantly rising from his comfortable position in the den, he made his way to the foyer to see who could possibly be visiting at this hour.

"Yes?" he said upon opening the door. Standing contritely in front of him was a very frazzled-looking Alvera. Her face was streaked with tears, and her breathing was heavy as if she had just sprinted all the way there. The master grew concerned. "Alvera. What is it? What's wrong?"

"My father's been shot."

"What?" he said, ushering her inside.

"It was my uncle. He showed up unexpectedly at our house this evening. When my father opened the door for him, he forced his way in and started yelling. My father tried to get him to leave, but he wouldn't, so my mother called the police. Then they got into a fight, and he pulled out a gun and shot him. My uncle's been captured, and an ambulance has already taken my father to the hospital. My mother's on her way there, but she sent me to come get you."

The master quickly tried to process what was happening. He knew what he needed to do, but should he go tell Felix? No. There wasn't time. He would just have to leave him a note. He didn't like doing that in a situation like this, but he didn't have a choice. Before he could put his plan into action, however, Alvera suddenly broke down in a flood of hysteria.

"What's going to happen?! Is he going to be all right?! Please, tell me he'll be all right! I don't want to lose him! P…please! Tell me…he'll…b…be…all right!"

"Alvera," the master gently said, kneeling down and grabbing her by the shoulders. "Alvera. Look. Look at me. Calm down. Listen. I don't know what's going to happen, but I do know that your father is in good hands and that you are too. I'm here for you, Alvera, and I promise. I'll stay with you and your mother as long as you need me, but I need you to be brave. All right?"

She nodded and began to wipe her face with her sleeve.

"Sir, what's going on down there?"

Master Marlow turned and saw the half-asleep butler, still dressed in his striped pajamas and stocking cap, groggily tottering down the stairs. He stopped at the bottom when he saw Alvera and grew considerably more alert.

"Alvera? What are you…" His words failed as he noticed the tears still pouring down her reddened cheeks. He looked with concerned confusion from the crying girl to the master as if he expected to find an explanation in one of their faces. "What happened?"

"Felix," the master said, stepping forward, "Alvera's father has just been shot."

"Oh, dear!"

"I'm going to ride with her to the hospital."

"Do you want me to go with you?"

"No, I need you to stay here and manage the house. I don't know how long I'll be gone, but I'll call you when I'm heading back."

"All right, Sir. Be safe."

He nodded. "Come on, Alvera."

The two friends hurried out the front door and around to the back of the house. The horses had already settled down in their stalls for the night, but when he saw his master, Obsidian sprang to his hooves, fully alert. As soon as Master Marlow had finished harnessing him with the reins, he helped Alvera into the saddle and then hoisted himself up in front of her.

"Hold on tightly," he said over his shoulder. Alvera responded by wrapping her stringy arms around his waist. The master leaned forward. "All right, Sid," he whispered in the horse's ear. "To the hospital, as fast as you can go. Yah!"

With a snap of the reins and a sharp kick in the sides, Obsidian reared slightly before lunging into a full-on gallop. It was the fastest he had ever gone before. He must have sensed the urgency in his master's tone and actions.

When they arrived at the hospital, they found Alvera's mother standing in the waiting area, conversing with a doctor and a couple of nurses. They listened from a distance while they waited for them to finish.

"Your husband is being prepared for surgery as we speak," the doctor said. "Depending on where the bullet is lodged in his chest, he may or may not make it, but I assure you … we will do everything we can. My assistant, Charlene, will keep you updated on his condition," he said, indicating the nurse to his left. "In the meantime, please, make yourself comfortable, and don't hesitate to call if you need anything."

"All right," Anita said, nodding. "Thank you, Dr. Harvey."

He nodded back politely before vanishing down the hall with the two nurses. As soon as they were gone, Anita wiped her glossy eyes and approached her daughter and the master. They met her halfway. First, she hugged Alvera, and then, quite unexpectedly, she threw her arms around the master. He tried not to appear too uncomfortable as he gingerly returned the gesture. Stepping back, she attempted to smile at him.

"Mr. Marlow, thank you so much for coming on such short notice. I know it's late. I hope we didn't wake you."

"Oh, no. Not at all. Besides, I'm always happy to help as much as I can. I'm sorry about your husband."

"It's all right."

"How is he?"

"Well, I guess you heard a little of what the doctor was saying. He's in critical condition. They're preparing him for emergency surgery right now, but …" she shook her head as more tears pooled in her eyes, "it doesn't look good."

"I'm sorry."

She was silent for a moment before she lifted her freckled face, now painted with her pent-up tears, and said, "I guess all we can do now is pray."

"Yes."

After offering the grieving woman a handkerchief, the master gently put his arm around her shoulders and led her over to a grouping of sofas where Alvera was already seated. He sat down next to her, and Anita sat on the couch perpendicular to theirs.

For the next two hours, all was deathly quiet, except for the elevator music softly humming from the overhead speakers and the various televisions tuned in to news, comedy, and home renovation channels. They seemed to be the only living things left in the entire building. The master hadn't seen anyone walk by in quite some time. The nurse also hadn't come to give them an update on Mr. Levlen's condition yet either, but that wasn't out of the ordinary. For surgeries, updates usually weren't given until after the procedure, and the master knew from experience that some surgeries could take several hours to complete, especially one as serious as this.

What *was* out of the ordinary was Alvera. In all this time, she hadn't moved a millimeter. She just sat there with eyelids half closed, staring off into a world that was somewhere between waking and sleeping, reality and fantasy, life and death. It was as if she had turned into a statue of herself, mute and deaf to everything and everyone around her. In her attempt to process everything that was happening, she had cut herself off from the world, including the master, and he could feel the distance growing between them.

He ventured a glance at her. Physically, she was only a few inches from him, but mentally, she was miles away. Yet, the master felt as if he had been to the same place. It was both warm and cold. Soothing and harsh. Tranquil and chaotic. It had the power to lull one into a dreamless sleep or catapult one into a relentless nightmare. Yes! He had been there. It was that secluded cove on the beach. The one he and Alvera had visited in the summer. When they had sat side by side on the shore, watching the sun pour its indigo, magenta, crimson, and tangerine oils into the ocean as it set. Only, this time, their roles were reversed. Instead of the master needing comforting, it was Alvera who needed it, but he wasn't exactly sure how to provide it. He was still a novice in that area.

While he struggled to come up with some ideas, he let

his gaze wander up to Alvera's face. He had never seen her look so solemn before, not even when she was homesick. Her jaw was rigidly set in place. A concerned crease almost seemed to be permanently glued to her forehead, and tears appeared to be frozen on the edges of her eyelashes. It was taking all the strength and courage she had just to hold her cracking vase of emotions together. The master's heart ached to see her suffering so. She didn't have to try so hard to keep it from him. Then again, he had done the same thing on the beach. He wondered if he had looked just as pained. He probably had. After all, he had certainly felt that way. That last thought gave him the inspiration he needed. He knew what to do.

In the midst of floundering in the paralyzing waters of her jumbled thoughts, Alvera suddenly felt a warmth that began to thaw her icy barrier. Eventually, it completely penetrated those frigid waters all the way to her heart and mind, and out of sheer curiosity, she turned to see where it was coming from. Master Marlow had laid his hand against her arm. She stared at it for a moment before looking up at his face. One corner of his mouth twitched up and gave her half a smile. She didn't return it. Pulling his arm away and opening it up, he invited her to come closer. She still didn't move. She just kept staring like a teary-eyed toddler lost in a store. But then, the last piece of stubborn ice melted, causing the vase to shatter, and all her racing emotions burst forth in a tsunamic wave. As if she were being propelled by its surging crest, Alvera flung herself into the master's arms, clutched at his shirt, and sobbed into his chest. He folded one arm around her back and cradled her head with the other before resting his cheek against the top of her golden head. It was soft and smelled of the crisp night wind. As he breathed in its haunting scent and listened to the chilling whine of her muffled tears, he fervently prayed that her father would be all right. He had to be. For her sake.

21

Alvera's eyes fluttered open, and the first thing they saw, once they had adjusted to the piercing brightness of the florescent hospital lights, was the master's face smiling down at them from above.

"Good morning," he said.

She blinked confusedly at him a few times before remembering where she was. However, she didn't remember being in a horizontal position. She looked around. Her face suddenly flushed tomato red as she realized what had happened: she had fallen asleep in the master's lap. She began to squirm uncomfortably as she tried to sit up. Seeing her embarrassment, the master helped her by gently pushing against her back. Once she was upright, she sheepishly scooted onto the cushion next to him and brushed a strand of loose hair back behind her ear.

"I'm sorry," she said after awkwardly staring down at her lap for a few seconds.

"Oh, no, you don't have to apologize, Dear. You were tired. Besides, you know I don't mind. You're light as a feather."

Some of her blush abated, and she managed to smile briefly at the master before turning serious once again. "Have they said anything?"

"Yes. Your father made it through the surgery and is in recovery. Right now, they're monitoring him for a little bit just to make sure his condition remains stable before they move him into a room, but they'll let us know when they do."

Alvera's entire body visibly relaxed as it was doused with relief. Her father was going to be all right. Thank goodness. Just then, the nurse appeared carrying a clipboard.

"Mrs. Levlen?" she called.

"Yes?" Anita answered, anxiously spinning around in her seat.

"Your husband has been moved to a room. I can take you to him if you'd like."

"Oh, yes! Thank you so much!"

"My pleasure, Ma'am."

Anita motioned to Alvera and Master Marlow, and they all stood and followed the nurse down the hall. They stopped at the elevator. Once they were all inside, the nurse pressed the button for the second floor. Stepping out onto the landing, they turned to the right into another hall. About half-way down, the nurse paused at an open door marked 214 and knocked.

"Mr. Levlen. It's Charlene. I've brought your family here to see you."

There was a faint reply within. The nurse then entered, followed closely by her party of three. They were met with the soft, rhythmic beeping of a heart monitor. Tracing the sound to the far side of the room, they found Mr. Levlen partially reclined in his bed. He looked as if he had just woken up from the sedation. Purple shadows swam beneath his eyes, but they appeared to be almost black against the sickly pallor of his skin. The only part of him that wasn't pale was his chest. Thankfully, most of it was covered up by a large patch of gauze. Master Marlow was sure he felt worse than he looked, but if he did, he didn't show it. In fact, he even managed to smile at them.

As soon as Anita saw that, her eyes sparkled with tears of joy, and she hurried over to her husband's side. "Oh, Kirk!" she said, gently smoothing his disheveled hair and kissing him on the forehead. Alvera joined them, and her father extended his hand to her. She clasped it in her own hands for a few moments before he reached up and touched her cheek.

While the reunited family continued to fellowship in this manner, Master Marlow simply stood back and took it all in. They had such a strong bond, much like the one he shared with Alvera, yet there was something different. There was a connection unlike anything he had ever seen or felt before. He couldn't explain it. He couldn't comprehend it. It was just so unique, so intimate, so…beautiful, and suddenly, he found his heart longing for it as well. But the longing only caused him pain when he realized that it was just another one of his seemingly unattainable dreams. It wasn't something that Alvera, her family, or anyone else could provide. It had to come from his own family, and that was a bond that had been broken a long time ago. True, he had rebuilt most of it over the past few months, but he feared that the damage between him and Andrew was far too extensive to ever be repaired. He had tried, but every time he felt like he was finally making progress, his brother knocked down all his hard work, and he had to start completely over.

Nevertheless, he had to keep persevering just like Michael said. It had to be making a difference, even if it was a small one. That thought eased some of his pain. Perhaps his dream was not so unattainable after all.

Just then, the family reunion was interrupted by the nurse. She came over to check the monitors and other equipment one more time to make sure that Mr. Levlen's vitals were still stable and that everything was hooked up correctly and working properly. After she finished, Mr. Levlen thanked her and then turned toward the master.

"And thank you, Mr. Marlow, for being here."

He nodded.

"I don't know what we ever…" He moved the wrong way and winced in pain.

The master drew closer. "No, no. It's all right, Mr. Levlen. Just take it easy. You don't have to say anything else. This isn't about me. I'm just glad that you're all right."

"I thought I heard a nauseatingly familiar voice."

Master Marlow cringed inwardly and suddenly became sick to his stomach at the sound of those taunting words. He closed his eyes as a cloud of dread began to billow up in his chest. *No. Please, no.* Footsteps echoed through the doorway, but the master didn't turn to see who they belonged to. He didn't have to.

"Well, if it isn't my brother, Malformed," Andrew said

in his mocking cheerfulness as he came up alongside the master. "Scarring more lives, I see?"

Ignoring that last comment, Master Marlow acknowledged his brother as politely as he could and proceeded to introduce him to Alvera's family. He just hoped no one had heard the mispronunciation of his name or noticed the malevolent intentions behind his brother's scathing words. "Andrew, this is Anita and Kirk Levlen. Mr. and Mrs. Levlen, this is my brother, Andrew."

"So, this is the famous Levlen family," Andrew said, approaching Anita and chivalrously kissing her hand. "It's a pleasure to finally meet you."

"Oh…well…it's a pleasure to finally meet you as well, Mr. Andrew," Anita stuttered, quite taken aback. "Alvera's told us so much about you."

"Really?" he said, shooting Alvera a look that made her squirm. "Well, I guess there's really not much of a need for introductions then, is there? Ah, Mr. Kirk," he said facing the hospital bed. "It's wonderful to make your acquaintance as well, although I'm terribly sorry to see you in this condition. What happened if you don't mind my asking?"

"He was shot," Anita answered for him.

"Yes," the nurse chimed in, "and if that bullet had been one centimeter closer to his heart, he wouldn't have made it. You're a very lucky man, Mr. Levlen."

"Indeed," agreed Andrew. "Well, I certainly hope you have a quick recovery."

"Thank you," Kirk whispered weakly.

Andrew nodded before turning to Alvera. "Oh, Alvera." He patted her head. "You poor little thing. I'm so sorry you're going through all this as well, but," he leaned in closer and lowered his voice, "you know, it could have been avoided if you hadn't rejected my help. I tried to warn you about my brother's curse. Nevertheless, my offer still stands if you should ever change your mind."

Those words were only intended for Alvera, but she wasn't the only one who heard them.

"Don't talk to her like that."

Everyone instantly looked at Master Marlow. Their eyes were blinding lamps, trapping the master in the exposing rays of a spotlight. He suddenly felt as if he were confined in an uncomfortably small room, waiting to be interrogated for some heinous crime he didn't commit, but at that moment, he was willing to endure such a torturous feeling. If Andrew wanted to continue to bully and manipulate him, fine. But he wasn't going to let him do that to anyone else.

Andrew crossed his arms and leaned toward Anita. "Ooo! Jealous of his little pet, isn't he?"

"Andrew." The master discreetly motioned for his brother to come here. He did so with a smirk and a swagger in his step. When they were face to face, Master Marlow looked Andrew imploringly in the eye and whispered, "Please. Not here. Not now."

"Why not?" his brother sneered.

His words were baited, and they reeked of the sulfuric spice of anger. Once again, his brother was looking for a fight, and once again, the master wasn't going to give in. So, they just continued to stare into each other's eyes. The master's were soft like the silky surface of freshly brewed coffee, begging for mercy or even the slightest bit of restrained civility. They trembled and shimmered as they earnestly searched for those qualities in the chestnut spheres before them, but they were not to be found. Andrew's eyes were as tough as petrified wood and had about as much feeling as that lifeless timber too. A person seeking healing sap there would only come back with a heart full of splinters. There was no reasoning with him. He was far too stubborn. However, he could be challenged.

Steeling himself against the counterattack that was sure to follow, Master Marlow calmly yet deliberately asked, "What are you even doing here?"

His innocent question received an unexpected response. Andrew's haughty spirit instantly evaporated to reveal a stony foundation. His face became lifeless and gray, and every feature, from his eyebrows to his lips, hardened into an ugly snarl. However, his eyes were still very much animated. Hate quivered in their pits like a flame that could either explode or be extinguished at any minute. The master thought the former was more likely to happen. After all, it was the same savage look his brother had given him just before he had attacked him that night in the snow. Well, at least they were in a hospital this time.

Andrew took a step forward, but the master stood his ground. They were so close now that their noses were nearly touching, and the master could feel his brother's molten breath scorching his skin. As they silently faced off in this dual for dominance, Andrew spat in his most deadly whisper, "None of your business," roughly bumped past his brother, and dramatically stalked out of the room.

Master Marlow watched his angry figure hasten down the hall before turning back to Alvera and her family. They too had been watching his brother's every move, but now, their gazes rested on him. They looked like a cluster of terrified bunnies that had huddled together during a vicious fight between two foxes. It was as if they were expectantly waiting for an explanation to all the violence, but the master didn't have one. He thought that he had been an innocent victim just like everyone else in this situation, but in reality, he was no better than his brother. Instead of avoiding a scene, he had been the key agent to creating one and a rather uncouth spectacle of himself at the same time. He couldn't bear to know what Alvera's parents thought of him now. He was no more than a target of abuse, and no matter what he did, every time he was hit, someone else always got hurt. Ashamed, he hung his head.

"I'm sorry," he said after a stretch of strained silence. "Please, excuse me for a moment."

Without looking up even a millimeter, he hurriedly ducked out of the room. Just outside the door to the right, he leaned against the wall, tilted his head back, and closed his eyes. He didn't need to go far; he just needed enough space to create a barrier between him and the Levlens' accusatory eyes.

A few seconds later, he felt a presence to his left. Cautiously, he took a peek in that direction. Alvera had appeared in the doorway, and as soon as she spotted him, she joined him by his side. He lowered his head again. For several minutes, they just stood there, absentmindedly watching various doctors and nurses walk by, until Alvera finally worked up the courage to speak.

"What are you doing?"

"I just…needed to step out for a moment. That's all."

"Mr. Marlow, you have nothing to feel guilty about. You didn't do anything wrong."

He hesitated. "I just feel bad about always dragging you and your family into my messes."

"It's ok. They know."

He looked at her with surprise.

"My parents," she explained. "I told them about Andrew. They understand."

Yes, he supposed they did. How could he forget? They were in an almost identical situation to his own. He wished that none of them were dealing with such issues, but knowing that they had that in common did make him feel a little better.

Seeing him smile, Alvera asked, "So, are you ready to come back?"

He paused. "You go ahead."

Her hopefulness faded.

"I'll be back in a few minutes," he added. "I promise."

Alvera wasn't completely reassured that he was all right, but she did as she was told and rejoined her family. As soon as she was out of sight, the master began scanning the hall. Ever since his brother's abrupt departure, he had been thinking. His sudden change in demeanor and defensive response to his question had made him curious. He was pretty sure he knew what it was all about, but it never hurt to investigate. Spotting a nurse who had stopped to plug in some data into a computer at a nearby station, the master made his move.

"Excuse me," he said approaching her. "I'm not sure if you can help me. I'm looking for a Brenda."

"Brenda Hobbs?" She turned and pointed a short way down the hall. "Room 220."

"Thank you."

He made his way to the door and knocked.

"Come in," chimed a sweet voice from within.

He entered and closed the door behind him. The room was exceedingly dark, especially at the entrance, for all the lights had been turned off. Brenda must have been resting.

"Andrew?" she said as he advanced further into the room. "I know you said you'd come back, but I didn't think it would be this soon. Did you forget something?"

Master Marlow hesitated before stepping into what little light was seeping in through the half-closed blinds. As soon as the bleached rays chased away the shadows that had been obscuring his face, Brenda's cheerful countenance fell and was replaced with a slight flush of embarrassment.

"Oh! I'm terribly sorry! I thought you were my fiancé."

Ouch! What a blow! As much as the master didn't like being compared to his brother, he couldn't deny it. They did look a lot alike. They always had. After all, both of them took after their father, and that wasn't something the master was particularly proud of either.

Shaking off the unintended insult as best he could, he forced himself to smile. "It's all right. You must be Brenda."

"Yes. And you are?"

"I…" The master caught himself just in time. He

couldn't give Brenda his real name, for if word ever got back to Andrew that he had spoken to her, let alone seen her, he would be a dead man for sure. But he didn't want to blatantly lie to her either. Suddenly, he remembered the nickname that Pete always called him. It would work. "I'm Dr. Mal."

After they shook hands, Master Marlow sat down in a chair positioned at the foot of the bed. Brenda placed her hands back in her lap and smiled sadly down at them.

"Hmph. I guess the other doctor couldn't figure out what was the matter with me either?"

"Well…what does seem to be the matter?"

"I was born with a rare immune deficiency disease. Of course, that means I'm more prone to illness than other people, but I'm also affected more severely than people with different immune deficiencies. In fact, it's not uncommon for me to be sent to the hospital every one or two months."

"What sent you here this time?"

"Fortunately, it was just a cold this time. You should have seen me when I had bronchitis. It was so bad that the doctors didn't think I was going to make it."

Now, that was exceedingly strange. Most people who got bronchitis had allergies, suffered from asthma, or were smokers, and even in those cases, it usually wasn't deadly. The master scrutinized Brenda for a moment. She had to be in her forties, but she certainly didn't look it. Her face was so youthful. It was like a flawless oil painting framed in chocolate curls. Hardly any lines aged her smooth skin, except for a couple of tired bags hanging beneath her eyes. And those eyes! Breathtaking. They were the deepest shade of blue he had ever seen. They reminded him of the ocean. She looked so healthy, yet she was so sick. Just what kind of immune deficiency did she have? The master's gaze roamed to the foot of the bed and saw a clipboard hanging from a nail.

"Do you mind if I take a look at your chart?" he asked, reaching for it.

"Not at all."

While he perused the pages of information scribbled with various names, contacts, medications, and notes, Brenda rambled on.

"No one's really sure what they can do for me anymore. They've only ever had one other patient with this disease, and he died before the doctors could gain a full understanding of it. They've tried giving me different medications to strengthen my immune system, but none of them seem to do anything for me. Nothing seems to work."

Her voice trailed away like an echo within the sterile walls of the room. Master Marlow was still busily scanning the chart, but he had heard every word she had said. He combined her additional information with what he had learned and fed it into the gears of his mind. They cranked and whirled at incredible speeds for several minutes until the master jerked his head up, his eyes flashing with an idea. They were met with Brenda's earnest gaze. It was as if she sensed that he had figured something out.

"So. Can you help me?"

He didn't want to get her hopes up too much, so he simply said, "I don't know. But I will do what I can."

She nodded before being seized by a few dry coughs.

The master stood preparing to leave. "So, when do you think you'll get to go home?"

"Tomorrow. The doctors want to keep me one more night just to make sure my fever doesn't flare back up."

The master grew concerned. There was something off in her tone. "You don't sound too happy about that."

"What? Oh, no! I'm very happy to be going home. I just have other things on my mind."

"What things?"

"My fiancé." She sighed. "I just don't know what to do."

Master Marlow blushed. He had taken this too far. "I…I'm sorry. I didn't mean to pry into something so personal."

"No, no. It's all right. To be honest, I've been needing to talk to someone about this."

Their eyes met, and the master grew even more uncomfortable. He suddenly wished that he hadn't even considered this investigation. Perhaps he could get out of it by telling Brenda that he had somewhere else he had to be. After all, he did need to get back to Alvera and her family.

But before he could even form the first word of his excuse, Brenda softly asked, "Is it all right if you're that someone?"

It was a desperate cry for help, and it instantly melted the master's heart. He couldn't leave her now. She needed someone to listen, and even though they had just met, she trusted him enough to tell him her troubles. Perhaps they were part of a secret that she had been forced to keep for so long that she just had to get it off her chest. The master certainly knew what that felt like. Resolving to help, he nodded, and Brenda began her confession.

"Andrew and I…we've been engaged for six years now. We still get together as often as my health will allow, but it's just not the same as it used to be. He's changed. He used to smile whenever he saw me, but now, he seems so serious, so business-like. It's as if he's always in a hurry to be anywhere other than where I am. Like he's repulsed by me. He won't even look me in the eye anymore, and he never talks about our marriage. He's just become so secretive and aloof." She sighed. "I love him, but…sometimes I wonder if he still loves me. What do you think?"

Master Marlow grabbed his chin in his hand and thought for a long time. It was a difficult question to answer. He knew almost nothing about their relationship, but he did know a lot about Andrew. Much more than she needed to know. He glanced at a small table with a flat, circular top in the corner next to her bed. A dainty ring glittered dully on its gray surface. Brenda was at a crossroad in her life. How the master answered would determine which way she would go.

Taking a deep breath, he slowly walked to the side of her bed and gently clasped both of her hands in his. She never once took her eyes off his. "Well…I don't know much about love, but I do know this. If Andrew has stayed with you this long, his love for you is not gone. He probably just doesn't know how to express it. Besides, I'm sure it's hard for him to see you like this."

"I know. And that's another thing. I don't want to be a burden to him."

"If he truly loves you, you won't be."

A glowing smile slowly spread across Brenda's entire face.

"You're right. Thank you, Dr. Mal."

He nodded and headed toward the door just as she began to cough again.

"You know," she said once her fit subsided, "you really do resemble Andrew. You two could be brothers."

The master paused in the act of opening the door and chuckled silently. She didn't know how close to the truth she was.

"Maybe the next time I'm in the hospital you'll get to meet him."

"Maybe, but hopefully there won't be a next time. Stay well, Brenda."

"I'll try."

22

Two weeks had passed, and during that time, things finally seemed to calm down for everyone. Alvera's father got to go home from the hospital, and the master had no further run-ins with his brother. Everything was back to normal, and while the master appreciated the peace that it afforded, part of him missed the thrill of all the unexpected adventures of late. They had become such a regular part of his routine that now he almost didn't know what to do with himself. But he had better be careful. If he couldn't find something to do, Felix would find something for him, so the master decided to occupy his spare time with his letters.

Sitting in the den, he prepared to read Alvera's latest correspondence.

Dear Mr. Marlow,

You won't believe what happened! We went to see my uncle during visiting hours. I was so nervous. I didn't know what to expect. As you know, we didn't exactly part on good terms the last time we met. I was afraid

*that this meeting would just end in another confronta-
tion, but it didn't! As soon as my uncle saw my father,
he burst into tears. He was so happy to see him alive
and well, for he thought that the shot had killed him.
He said that he had never meant to take things that
far. He was just so blinded by his anger that he had let
it get the best of him.*

*My father forgave him, and then, the most in-
credible thing of all happened. They hugged each other!
I can't remember the last time I saw them do that. I
think their relationship is stronger now than it ever
was before. Of course, my uncle is still in jail, but we
promised him that we would visit him as often as we
could. Maybe one day he'll have a chance for parole. I
hope the same thing can happen with you and Andrew.*

Love,
Alvera

Master Marlow gave a melancholy sigh as he finished
reading. Of course, he was happy for Alvera and her family, but at the same time, he couldn't help but feel a little
twinge of jealousy. Just as Alvera had said, he too wished
for the same thing with Andrew. It seemed to have happened so quickly for her. Why couldn't it happen that way
for him? He took a deep breath and released it. *How can
you think that?* he chided himself. It hadn't been a short
and simple road for them. How many years had they been
dealing with this? And here he had only been in the same
situation for a few months. Still, it didn't make it any easier.

And then there was Brenda. Ever since he had met her in the hospital, the master had been feverishly working on something that would finally be able to help her. He had developed a treatment that would allow her to live a normal life and might even eventually cure her of her disease altogether. There was just one problem. He couldn't give it to her without Andrew finding out that he knew about his secret. True, this could be the needle that mends their relationship, but it could also be the bomb that destroys what little connection they have left. Everything depended on Andrew's ultimate decision. So, for the time being, all the master could do was continue to write and pray.

* * *

Master Marlow pulled Obsidian to a stop at the top of a hill that overlooked the town just outside his mother's neighborhood. He had left her house much later than he had intended. The sun was already beginning to set. However, he didn't mind taking a little time to enjoy its beauty, for since he was going to be late getting home anyway, there was no need to rush. Like a ruby, fragmenting rosy light in all directions, that magnificent ember fanned the last of its fiery rays over every inch of the unsuspecting town below. They seemed to ignite everything they touched. Shingled rooftops glittered like heaped up mounds of coals. Burgundy bricks burned as brightly as red-hot irons. Marble columns blushed as delicately as stacks of pale rose quartz, and every street glowed like rushing rivers of lava. The entire town had been transformed into an enchanting city of fire that flared majestically against the peachy sky, and to complete the royal backdrop, lavender clouds lazily draped themselves like kingly capes over the peaceful scene.

The warm radiance of it all brought a contented smile to the master's face. However, it suddenly faded when he spotted a particularly large cloud billowing up from the horizon. Only, it wasn't a cloud; it was a plume of smoke. Something really was on fire in the town.

"Come on, Sid," the master said, sitting up in the saddle and tightening his grip on the reins. "Let's go check it out." He dug his heels into Obsidian's sides, and the two took off in a gallop.

Everything blurred to the master's vision as they zigzagged through the maze of streets. His eyes were solely focused on the beacon of smoke, for it and the distant sirens were his only guides. Fortunately, he didn't have to pay much attention to his surroundings since most people had already gone home from work. There were only a few straggling pedestrians, a handful of cars, and a couple of reckless taxi drivers that they had to dodge. Other than that, their path was pretty clear.

Soon, the master noticed that Obsidian's sleek coat and mane were beginning to be peppered with specks of gray and white. He felt the same powdery flakes pelting his face. It was snowing ash. They were getting close. Rounding two more corners, they finally arrived at the source. It looked like someone had started a giant bonfire. A multiple-story brick building was completely engulfed in flames. Even several buildings away, one could feel the intense heat pulsating from its charred walls, but not Master Marlow. All he could feel was the clammy numbness of horror dripping down his limp arms and legs. "Oh, no," he breathed. He knew the building. It was the law firm where Andrew worked. And he also knew that Andrew hadn't come home yet. Obsidian felt his master's hold weaken, slowed down, turned his head, and whinnied. It jolted the master back to reality. *You're jumping to conclusions again,* he chided himself. *I'm sure he's fine. I'm sure of it. I'm sure.* Pushing the rest of his fears behind him for the moment, he urged Obsidian onward.

From a safe distance away, he tied his faithful companion to a tree and cautiously approached the blazing structure. Two firetrucks were positioned on either side. One firefighter at the top of each ladder aimed water at the upper flames to keep them at bay, while several others manned two massive hoses on the ground. Four ambulances were parked a short distance up the street to the left and were already busy loading up some of the wounded. In between, the rest of the street was swarming with businessmen and women. The more severely injured were either sitting or lying on the ground while those that were still able rushed about trying to do anything they could to help. Of course, some of them were too hysterical to be of any use. Their manic cries clashed with the cacophony of groans, shouts, wailing sirens, gushing water, and roaring flames that thundered all around them. It was absolute chaos, and the master was heading right into the middle of it. But as he drew closer, one of the firemen hurried toward him.

"Excuse me, Sir," he said, stopping him from advancing any further. "I'm sorry, but I'm going to have to insist that all civilians keep a safe distance away. This is a very dangerous situation."

"I understand, but I'm not a civilian. I'm Dr. Malchus Marlow. I saw the smoke as I was passing through this area, and I came to see if there was anything I could do to help."

"Well, as you can see, a medical staff is already on the scene. I appreciate your concern, Dr. Marlow, but ..."

"Wait!"

They both turned and saw a man jogging toward them. His suit was disheveled and covered with soot. Ash was smeared all over his sweaty face and hands, and a streak of dried blood stretched from the top of the left side of his head down to his cheek.

"You're a doctor?" he panted, trying to catch his breath.

"Yes."

"Oh, thank goodness! We've got several people over there who need immediate medical attention. The ambulances have already taken some to the hospital, but there aren't enough to get the rest of them. They're having to make multiple trips. Do you think you can help us?"

Master Marlow looked at the firefighter. He nodded his approval. Turning back to the desperate man, the doctor said, "I'll see what I can do."

"All right. This way. Follow me."

They sped toward the jumbled crowd. As they did so, the master couldn't help but anxiously scan every grimy face as it came into focus. There were dozens and dozens of law firm workers, but Andrew was not among them. His fears drifted back to the forefront of his mind.

"Is this everyone?" he called out to his guide.

"I think so."

"No," someone sputtered to the right.

They stopped and saw two firefighters supporting a man that they had just rescued from the smoldering building. The man's clothes and skin were severely burned. He coughed before finishing what he had to say.

"There's still one more trapped in the office on the top floor."

The master's heart skipped a beat. *No. Please, no. It can't be.* He was almost too afraid to ask, but he had to know.

"Do you know who it is?"

"I…I think his name is Andrew." He coughed again. "Andrew Marlow."

"No," the master whispered. He felt the same icy numbness wash over him that he had felt when he first sighted the building. It seemed to paralyze his entire body. He couldn't move or even breathe. All he could do was stare at those fiendish flames as they mocked him in slow motion. However, their taunting quickly ignited his adrenaline. It exploded into his system, shocking everything back to life. He could feel its electrifying pulses in every shuddering breath, which in turn fueled the rest of his body with quivering energy. But it was so powerful of a surge that it worked his mind into a frenzy. All rational thinking was gone. Only impulse remained, and before the master could process what he was doing, he lunged toward the building. "NO!!"

The two firemen immediately tackled him to prevent him from plunging into the consuming fire.

"Steady, man!" one of them said.

The master frantically struggled against their restraining grasp. "No! Andrew!"

More people came to the firemen's aid.

"Let me go! I have to save him!"

They each tried to dissuade the master from his suicidal mission in turn.

"Have you gone mad?!"

"Don't be daft!"

"That place is a deathtrap!"

"You'll never make it out alive!"

But their words only caused the master to fight with even more determination to break free. "No! That's my brother!"

"Dr. Marlow!" said the businessman who had initially recruited the doctor's help. He scurried around the knotted group until he was standing directly in front of him. Placing his hands on his buckling shoulders, he looked directly into the master's wild eyes. They were moist with … the man couldn't tell if they were drops of sweat or tears, but it didn't matter. "Listen. The fire department is doing everything they can. Two men are in there right now looking for your brother. I promise that you'll be the first person to be informed as soon as they know something, but you're not going to do anyone any good if you go in there. We need you out here." He pointed to the cluster of injured men and women scattered on the ground. "They need you."

The master let his words sink in, and slowly, they restored his sanity. He was right. It was foolish of him to rush in like that. There was nothing he could do for his brother right now. If he really wanted to help, he needed to focus on the issue at hand.

Nodding and swallowing to suppress his emotions, he calmly said, "All right."

As soon as the gathered mob released him, he wiped his eyes on the back of his sleeve and made his way to the wounded. They were grouped by the severity of their injuries. The worst cases were treated first. Most of them had second or third-degree burns, but a few had further complications such as broken bones and enormous gashes that needed to be stitched. There were even a couple of people who had gone into a state of shock. Those with minor injuries only had a few mild burns and scrapes.

With each patient, the master worked quickly yet thoroughly. In fact, he only had a handful of people left to treat when there was a commotion at the entrance of the building. The sooty businessman suddenly came running up to him.

"Dr. Marlow! They found him! They found your brother!"

Master Marlow immediately dropped his medical supplies, sprang to his feet, and sprinted toward the huddled group of firemen that had formed in front of the law firm, his heart pounding in his ears. They parted to let him through. Lying unconscious on a stretcher on the ground was his brother.

"How is he?" the master asked as he kneeled down to examine him more closely.

"He's alive, but barely," said one fireman.

"We found him pinned beneath a beam that had collapsed from the roof," another chimed in.

"He has severe third-degree burns and has breathed in a lot of smoke," said a third.

The master identified each injury as they named it. Andrew's breathing was exceedingly shallow and laborious from all the smoke in his lungs, and nearly three-fourths of his body was covered in burns. But the worst part was his right leg. It had been burnt so badly that it was almost as black as the master's hair, and now, it was beginning to leak fluid profusely. It was clear that that was where he had been pinned. And it was that wound that would determine whether he lived or died.

The master abruptly stood up. "Get him in an ambulance," he said with a new sense of authority to two medics standing to the side of the group. "I'll meet you at the hospital."

With that, he raced back to Obsidian, untied him from the tree, mounted him, and tore off up the street as fast as he could.

23

A steady throbbing in his ears. At first, he thought it was just his heart, but after concentrating on it for several minutes, he slowly began to realize that it was something outside himself, something audible. A faint beep. It seemed to echo from a great distance away like a friend calling to him from the opposite side of a canyon. He had to find the source, but it was impossible to tell which direction it was even coming from. Sometimes it was in front of him. Sometimes to the right. To the left. Behind him. And sometimes it even seemed to come from all those directions at once. He blindly stumbled through the darkness, not knowing where he was going, what he was following, or if he were even following it at all. It seemed to him that he wasn't getting anywhere, for the landscape never changed. All he could see was the same black, formless void stretching on and on before him.

Eventually, however, he noticed that the darkness was somehow beginning to thicken and become more resistant to his efforts. So, he was making progress. He pushed against it. It was like rubber, flexible yet firm. He pushed harder, and it began to give. This was it. Whatever it was had to be on the other side of this barrier, and if he could just make it through, he would be free. With all his strength, Andrew gave one final shove, and the barrier snapped apart along with the darkness.

Light instantly flooded his eyes. Even though it really wasn't very bright, he had to blink a few times before he became accustomed to it. Everything seemed to be hidden in a fog, for he could only make out a few abstract shapes and blurred shadows. But even though his vision was impaired, his hearing was still functioning at its full capacity. The distant beeping that he had heard just moments before was now right next to him. He had found it. Only, it wasn't his alarm clock, as he had expected it to be. It sounded more like…a heart monitor? That didn't make any sense. After all, he was at home. Wasn't he?

Slowly, his surroundings came into focus, and he noticed a man dressed in a white lab coat standing a few feet away at a counter. He was slightly bent over something. But it wasn't just any man. Andrew could recognize that shoulder-length raven hair and hunched back anywhere.

"Malchus?" he croaked, squinting at him. "What are you doing here?"

"I'm a doctor. I'm doing my job."

He looked around, confused. "Where am I?"

"You're in the hospital."

"The hospital?"

"Yes. You were in a bad fire."

Andrew dug into the recesses of his clouded mind. Ah, yes. That was right. He remembered. With a sigh, he let his bandaged head fall back onto the pillow and stared up at the tiled ceiling.

"How long have I been here?"

"Almost twenty-four hours."

Laying a pencil aside that he had been using to scribble notes down on a clipboard, Master Marlow turned away from the counter and walked over to the bed. He gently lifted a clear bag off a metal rack and examined its contents. Andrew craned to see what it was, but it was just outside his peripheral vision.

"What's that?"

"An IV."

Satisfied with what he saw, the doctor replaced the bag on its hook and returned to his station at the counter to take down more notes. At this point, Andrew was getting a little perturbed by his brother's curt responses, for they weren't telling him anything. He wanted concrete answers, not obscure hints.

Clearing his throat, he said, "So, I suppose once I recover, I'll be back to normal." He waited for a reply, but none came. "Right?" he pressed a little more earnestly.

"Mostly."

That one word dispelled all his frustration and replaced it with an unsettling fear. Something was wrong. "What do you mean?" he warily asked.

The master stopped what he was doing, sighed, and hung his head. He knew this moment would come, but that didn't make it any easier. He slowly turned toward the bed, and for the first time since his brother regained consciousness, he looked him directly in the face. His chestnut eyes were ringed with dozens of questions, and the master could sense the dread that lurked behind each one. It hurt his heart to tell him the truth, but no matter how painful it was, he had to tell him.

"Andrew…" He hesitated briefly while he worked up the courage to continue. "When the firefighters pulled you out of the building, you were lucky to even be alive. You had been trapped beneath a beam, had inhaled a lot of smoke, and had sustained several serious burns, particularly on your right leg." He walked around to the right side of the bed and grabbed the sheets. "I'm just going to go ahead and warn you. You're not going to like what you see."

He pulled them down. Andrew was too stunned by what he saw to even react to his horrified surprise. Where his right leg should have been, there was nothing but blank mattress. All that remained of it was a swollen, knobby stump that didn't even reach down to his knee. It was strange. Even though it was gone, it still felt like it was there. While Andrew stared in disbelief, the master continued his explanation.

"I did everything I could. I really did, but the damage was too extensive. Your third-degree burns were so severe that they penetrated almost to the bone and were causing you to lose large amounts of vital bodily fluids. I had no choice. In order to save your life, I had to amputate your leg. However, your condition is only temporary. As soon as your wound has completely healed, we'll fit you for a prosthetic leg."

"Oh! What's the point?" his brother suddenly blurted before rolling his head defeatedly to the side. "It's over."

"Don't talk like that. It's not over. Yes, things will be different and painful at first, but once you build up your strength and tolerance, the pain will lessen, and you'll be able to do all the things you were able to do before."

"No! I won't! Look at me! Nothing is ever going to be the same! I'm never going to be normal again! I'm a freak!" That last word echoed vehemently around the room as Andrew stopped his ranting to catch his breath. With an exaggerated sigh, he laid his head back down, closed his eyes, and said in an alarmingly calm voice, "You should have let me die."

A long pause ensued in which the only sounds to be heard were the piercing beeps of the heart monitor and the wheezing pumps from the oxygen tank. Master Marlow didn't know what to say, but there really wasn't anything more to say. Words wouldn't help Andrew right now. All he could do was stand there and helplessly watch as his brother lay silently brooding over his own deplorable condition. In the midst of such self-pitying, however, Andrew abruptly broke into bitter laughter.

"Well," he began between chuckles, "I guess I finally know how you've felt all these years. Different. Abnormal. Deformed." He sighed again. "You should have let me die." A few moments later, his eyebrows (what was left of them) scrunched together. "No. Death would have been too good for me. Unlike you, I deserve this." His voice began to crack with emotion. "After all those years of teasing you, bullying you, attacking you…and especially after everything that has recently happened between us…I deserve this punishment." He swallowed a lump that threatened to choke him. "You never did anything to me, yet I continued to hate you." He couldn't hold it back any longer. Without warning, Andrew burst into tears and buried his face in his hands. "I'm sorry, Malchus! I'm so, so sorry! I wasn't a very good big brother to you! In fact, I was absolutely wretched! You deserved so much better than me!"

"Andrew," the master gently said, laying a hand on his trembling shoulders. "It's all right."

"No! No, it's not!" he gasped between aching sobs. "I don't deserve your forgiveness!"

"I'm not asking if you feel like you deserve it or not. I'm simply giving it to you."

"Why?!" he said, jerking his head in the master's direction. "After everything I've said…everything I've done…why?! Why did you even save me?!"

While he waited for an answer, Andrew's heart-rending cries quieted, and his red, watery eyes grew round with wonder. He couldn't believe or understand what he saw. Master Marlow's entire face began to glow like an angel the longer he gazed at his brother. Yes, his brother was a mess, from the waterfalls streaking his flushed face to the mucus that had begun to run down his oxygen tube, but there was still something about the whole scene that touched his heart and made him smile.

As tears brimmed up in his compassionate eyes, he quietly said, "Because…you're my brother, Andrew. And no matter what, I will always love you."

His simple words caused Andrew to sob even harder. Reaching into his coat, he pulled out a handkerchief and handed it to him. "Here. And I promise that it's clean."

Laughing and crying at the same time, his brother humbly accepted the gift.

24

Sitting on the edge of the hospital bed, Andrew finished fastening his prosthetic leg, stared at its metallic surface for a moment, and sighed. Today was the day. He had practiced taking it on and off for several days now, but this would be the first time he had ever attempted to walk on it. He had to admit, he was a little nervous. After all, this was a huge step (literally and figuratively) for him, and he wasn't quite sure how it would go or even what to expect.

A knock at the door distracted him from his qualms.

"Come in."

It opened to admit Master Marlow. As soon as he saw his brother, he smiled. "Are you ready?"

He nodded.

With a slight nod back, the master stepped to the side to allow a nurse with a wheelchair to pass by. She gave a cheerful greeting to Andrew as she pushed the chair over to his bed. After checking his prosthetic leg to make sure it was securely and properly attached, she helped him into his seat, wheeled him to the threshold of the door, locked the wheels in place, and gave him his instructions. All he had to do was walk to the end of the hall and back. It sounded much easier than it looked. Andrew's room was all the way at the far-right end of the hall, so essentially, he was having to walk the length of the entire building. True, he had walked it many times before, but that was with the support of crutches. Now, he would have to rely solely on the strength of his legs. His only security blanket was the wall railing that extended the full length of the hall on either side, but even it only offered a minimum amount of comfort since it was chopped up by doors, nursing stations, and other obstacles.

And those other obstacles were another concern of his, for some of them included people. Andrew was still extremely self-conscious about his altered appearance. He knew that the hospital staff was used to seeing things like this, but it still didn't keep some people, especially visitors, from staring. It made him feel so awkward and vulnerable. Two things that he wasn't used to feeling. When he had his crutches, he could easily speed through his daily exercises and return to the safety of his room to avoid prolonged embarrassment if he needed to. This time, however, there was no quick escape. He had a feeling that this walk was going to be painfully slow in more than one way. He began to understand why his brother sometimes wore that cape of his, for at that moment, he wished that he had one too.

Master Marlow noticed that his brother's knuckles were beginning to turn white from the strangling holds they had on the arms of the wheelchair. He glanced at his face. He had that look of utter terror in his eyes. The master understood his struggle and placed a hand on his shoulder. His muscles instantly relaxed under that reassuring touch.

Bending down, he gently whispered in his ear, "Don't worry about if anyone else is watching. You're not doing this for them. You're doing it for yourself, and I'll be right beside you, supporting you all the way if you need me to."

Andrew let the master's words sink in for a moment before nodding. Knowing that his brother was there for him boosted his confidence. He wouldn't have to do this alone. It was just the encouragement he needed.

Taking a deep breath, he pushed himself up onto his good leg, grabbed the railing to balance himself, and pivoted to the left. Now, he just had to take that first step. He tentatively swung his right leg in front and let its metal foot gently tap the ground. So far so good. He let go of the railing. Good. He was still standing. But when he transferred his weight, everything collapsed. A shooting pain zapped all his strength and sent him toppling forward. However, before his knee could even hit the ground, his brother caught him in his arms.

"I've got you."

He lifted him up and set him back on his feet. Once Andrew was steady again and had firmly wrapped his arm around his brother's shoulders, Master Marlow loosened his supportive grip, and the two of them hobbled the rest of the way down the hall and back together.

* * *

Laughter filled the oppressive hospital room and seemed

to brighten it even more than the golden glow of the corner lamp did. Night had fallen, but the master and Andrew still sat at the small table in his room, talking and playing cards. They had spent the entire evening in this manner.

"You know, it's funny," Andrew said, shuffling his hand. "These have been some of the worst yet most wonderful weeks of my life, and it's all because of this." He gestured toward his leg.

The master smiled. "I'm glad." Realizing how that must have sounded, he quickly tried to amend his statement. "I mean…I'm not glad that you lost your leg, but…"

His brother started laughing before he could even finish. "It's all right, Malchus! I know what you mean!"

A smile returned to the master's face. He was just relieved that Andrew had not taken what he had said the wrong way.

The last of his brother's chuckles ended with a sigh. "I just wish I had realized my foolishness sooner. All those wasted years…"

"They weren't wasted years," the master interrupted. "Don't ever think that. Everything happens in God's timing. He knew that we needed that time to grow and mature. It was to prepare us for hardships to come. Hardships that we weren't ready to face until now."

"Yes. But I still think you matured a whole lot more than I did."

"I don't know. You've matured a lot over these past few weeks."

"Oh? You mean in my ability to beat you at cards?" He

slapped his hand face up on the table. "Ha! A full set of aces!"

Master Marlow had no choice but to fold. As he did so, he laughed and shook his head. "You're just as bad as Michael."

"At what?"

"At picking the most inopportune moment to change the subject."

"I was just trying to lighten the mood."

"Yes. So was Michael when we went to the park and ... oh."

The master's voice faded along with his cheerful countenance. Andrew noticed and grew concerned.

"What?"

"Nothing."

"No, really. Tell me."

He hesitated. "I was just referring to the time Michael and I had our first snowball fight in the park, but I forgot that you wouldn't know about it because it was in one of my letters ... and ... well ... you burned them."

"What? I never burned your letters."

The master finally looked up from staring down at his lap. "You didn't?"

"No."

"But ... Michael told me that he saw you burning them in the fireplace."

"Oh," he said, drawing out the word. "No. He saw me burning the *envelopes* to your letters."

Master Marlow continued to stare incredulously at his brother. He couldn't believe what he was hearing. His heart began to swell with an overwhelming joy. It meant so much to him that his brother had not simply taken one look and discarded his letters like garbage as he had originally thought. He had cared enough to keep them, but why? Did he even read them?

Sensing his confusion, Andrew proceeded to explain. After all, his brother deserved to know. "You see…yes. Initially, when I first started receiving your letters, I did want to burn them. I was still just so full of anger and jealousy that I didn't want anything to do with you. But, for some reason, I thought better of it and decided to take my frustration out on the envelopes instead. I kept the letters in one of the top drawers of my desk in my office at work. And there they sat for months, multiplying and growing ever more difficult to ignore.

"One day…I don't know why…I finally decided to read them." He paused, grabbed his chin, and thought for a moment. "In fact, it was the day of the fire. Anyway, once I started reading them, I couldn't stop. They were just so thoughtful and…beautiful. It was as if you were right there in the room with me, taking the time to tell me all about your life. And you wrote to me as if to a close friend, for you never mentioned one negative thing about me. That's when I began to realize just how foolish, stubborn, and awful I had been. You had been trying to reach out and connect to me ever since you were a little boy, but like most big brothers, I labeled you as a nuisance and continually pushed you away. Well, not anymore. For the first time in my life, I wanted to set things right.

"Unfortunately, I was so wrapped up in the revelation

of it all that I didn't realize what was happening around me until I heard shouting. I ran to the door to see what was the matter, but when I went to open it, it was flaming hot. A fire had started, and I hadn't even noticed, but by that point, it had apparently spread throughout the entire building. I was going to try to escape through one of the windows, but before I could reach one, a beam fell from the roof and pinned me to the ground. Smoke quickly began to fill the room. I called for help while desperately trying to free myself, but before I knew it, I couldn't breathe, and everything went black. Of course, you know the rest."

Both were silent for a moment before the master broke the stillness with a sigh. "I'm sorry, Andrew. I did it again."

"Did what again?"

"I try to help people, but somehow, I always end up hurting them instead. My letters are the reason you lost your leg."

"No. This isn't your fault. Your letters changed my heart. If I had simply read them as you sent them to me, this wouldn't have happened. My stubborn pride is the only one to blame for my missing limb."

He was right. The master had to stop blaming himself for every bad thing that happened. After all, sometimes God used them to bring about the good, just like He did in this case. The master had done the right thing, and now, he was reaping the rewards.

Andrew suddenly sighed. "I just wish I still had your letters. You know. As a reminder."

His brother smiled. "It's all right. They served their purpose."

25

"You know, Andrew," Master Marlow began as they walked side by side down the street toward a small café, "you don't have to do this."

Without averting his firm forward gaze, his brother solemnly replied, "Yes, I do."

It had only been a couple of days since Andrew had been released from the hospital. Even though he still walked with a noticeable limp, his mobility had improved considerably. Still, the master did not deem today's venture wise. His brother was not yet strong enough physically or emotionally to handle what he planned to do, but of course, his stubborn nature wouldn't allow him to be talked out of it. He was determined to face what he felt was necessary, and he wanted his brother to be there with him. This was another issue. The master felt that this matter was a little too personal for an outsider to be a part of. He didn't want to get in the way or make things any more awkward than they were going to be. However, his brother had insisted that he come, so he wasn't about to let him down. He was willing to do whatever he could to support him. He just hoped that Andrew wasn't making a big mistake.

When they were directly in front of the café, they noticed someone sitting at one of the outside tables. It was Brenda. She was already here. There was no turning back now. After waiting for Andrew to grab onto his shoulder, Master Marlow helped him across the street. He stepped to the side once they reached the sidewalk, for as soon as Brenda saw her long-lost fiancé, she rushed over and threw her arms around him.

"Oh, Andrew!" she said, burying her face in his neck. "I've been so worried about you!" Letting her hands slide onto his shoulders, she stepped back, so she could look him in the face. "I heard about the fire at the law firm. Ever since then, I've been trying to get in touch with you, but I could never get you to answer the phone. I even went by your house a few times, but you were never there either. You don't know how relieved I was when you called yesterday." She reached a hand up and let it rest against his cheek as she anxiously scanned his grave face with her intensely blue eyes. "Where have you been? Are you all right?" Her gaze travelled down toward his feet. She jumped back, gasped, and covered her mouth with her hands when she finally noticed his leg. "What happened?!"

"I lost my leg in the fire."

"Oh, Andrew! I'm so sorry!"

"No, don't feel sorry for me," he said, avoiding her attempts to hug him again.

Brenda cast him a mixed look of hurt and confusion. She didn't understand. Skirting around her, Andrew limped his way over to the table, caught its smooth edge, turned, and looked back at her.

"Please, sit down. We need to talk."

She hesitated for a moment but did as she was told. After staring at the ground for several painfully long minutes trying to figure out how he was going to approach the subject, Andrew took a deep breath, let it out, and looked up.

"Brenda…I'm not the man you think you know. I've been avoiding you. And not just for these past few weeks, but for these past six years. There's a reason why I've kept putting off our marriage, and it's time you knew the truth.

"My family has always prided itself in perfection. It was a legacy that I wanted to continue, and so far, I had. I excelled in school, had a successful and well-paying career, and was admired by many people. All I needed was a wife to match. That's when I met you. You were smart, beautiful, charming, extremely witty, graceful, sophisticated…everything I could have ever hoped for in a woman. You were perfect, except for one thing: your illness. Ever since you told me about it, I've been torn between love and logic. Unfortunately, my flawed logic usually got the best of me because I was so concerned about my image. That's why I never introduced you to my family. I was embarrassed. I began to focus more on your deficiency as an inconvenience instead of on who you really were as a person. Something I was guilty of doing with my own brother."

He looked at the master, and Brenda followed his gaze until he began to speak again. "And…I'm ashamed to admit it…but there were times…especially when you were in the hospital…that I viewed you as nothing more than a burden. A useless weight that I was allowing to drag my good name down into the mud for no reason." His voice began to tremble. "But through it all, you've been so patient and understanding. You continued to love and give me the benefit of a doubt when I most certainly didn't deserve it. I have deceived you and made you wait for far too long, so now, I finally give you my answer."

Reaching into his pocket, Andrew pulled out a small navy-blue box, set it on the table, and pushed it toward Brenda. Her mouth opened and her eyes widened when she saw it. She recognized it. It was the box that had once held her engagement ring. She stared at it in this manner for a moment longer before looking back up at Andrew. His eyes were full of tears, and his whole body seemed to quiver with sorrowful remorse. He had to swallow a lump that had formed in his throat before he could continue.

"I am not worthy of your love. If you so wish, I release you from our engagement. You deserve a far better man than me. One who will treat you with the utmost care and respect, no matter what."

At that point, Andrew was shaking so violently that his crippled leg threatened to give out from under him. It was almost too painful to watch. The master felt that he needed to do something, but he didn't know what. Should he help him, or should he resist the urge to do so? Before he could make up his mind and before his brother completely lost his balance, Andrew tightened his grip on the table, lowered his head, and closed his eyes. He couldn't bear to look at Brenda's heartbroken face any longer, let alone when she made the decision.

For what seemed like hours, he waited for the divorcing snap of the box, but it never came. Then, he heard the soft shuffle of fabric as Brenda slid out of her chair. This was it. He squeezed his eyelids more tightly together, bracing himself for the inevitable. Seconds turned into minutes, but still nothing happened. The suspense was unbearable. What was she waiting for? Why didn't she just get it over with already?

Andrew jumped when something suddenly touched him. Slowly, he opened his eyes and turned his head toward his hand that was clenching the table. Brenda had placed both of hers on top of it, one of which still bore the ring he had given her. He couldn't contain his puzzling curiosity any longer. Lifting his head all the way, he found himself face to face with her. Compassionate tears sparkled in the fathomless depths of her eyes and reflected the apparent fear and surprise in his own along with the streaks now lining his cheeks. A smile trembled on her dainty lips. Gently lifting one of her hands, she reached up and brushed some of his watery stains away. As she did so, she lovingly whispered, "How can I deserve better when I already have the best?"

He couldn't believe it. After everything, she still loved him and wanted to be with him. It was too much. Overwhelmed by such Christ-like grace, Andrew threw himself onto her shoulder and completely broke down. Brenda, in turn, wrapped her arms around him and soothingly rubbed his back until his sniffling and sobbing abated. Then, they looked at each other and kissed. After they separated, Master Marlow approached, smiling. Brenda smiled back.

"I knew you two had to be brothers." She suddenly cast Andrew a questioning look. "How come you never told me you had another brother besides Michael?"

He chuckled as he wiped his face. "That's a long story."

"Yes," agreed the master, "and here's another one, but for now, I'll just give you the short version. I've developed a treatment that will improve Brenda's condition."

Both of them were speechless for a moment. Andrew tried to speak, but all that came out were fragments of incoherent sounds. And Brenda simply couldn't because this time she was the one who was crying. Eventually, however, they found their voices.

Clasping his fiancé excitedly in his arms, Andrew turned to his brother and said, "Thank you, Malchus!"

"Yes," Brenda beamed through tears, "thank you so much!"

* * *

Pale pink and white May blossoms crowded the tender, verdant boughs of the trees lining the street, and with every breeze, even if it were no more than a sigh, dozens of petals would take flight and shower passing vehicles and pedestrians like flurries of snow. A few of those silken sprites drifted in through one of the windows of Master Marlow's carriage and landed in his lap, bringing the delicate scent of sweet nectar with them. He closed his eyes and breathed it in. It was the same fragrance that had delighted his senses just moments before at Andrew and Brenda's wedding.

It was nothing extravagant. Just an intimate outdoor

wedding on the grounds of a church with the audience consisting of no more than the two immediate families and the Levlens. But that made it all the more special. Brenda had no siblings, so Alvera was elected to be the flower girl, Michael the ring bearer, and the best man was none other than Master Marlow himself. (Andrew had insisted.) He was honored to stand at his brother's side during one of the happiest moments of his life, and that honor rewarded him with a memory he would treasure forever.

Looking out from his vantage point, he could see all the smiling faces of his friends and family gathered together. There was Alvera in a white dress trimmed with lace, discreetly waving at him from her seat on the front row. Next to her, Felix and Michael both sat with their faces buried in handkerchiefs, and slowly drifting down the aisle was Brenda, glowing with new-found health and vitality. Everyone was proud of the new couple for overcoming all their struggles to get to this point, but none more so than the master's mother. Agatha's wish had finally come true. One of her sons was getting married. The master was glad that it was Andrew because he had already decided a long time ago that marriage wasn't for him, but that was all right. He already had everything he could ever need: faith, family, friends, and love.

He plucked one of the petals from his lap and thoughtfully rubbed its shimmery surface between his fingers. Spring. Like fall, it was another season of constant change, but unlike its autumnal cousin, it did not symbolize death and decay. It symbolized new life and new beginnings. And this was most certainly the beginning of a new life for the master. He looked out his window. A silver car was coming in the opposite direction. He smiled at the driver as she passed, and to his surprise, she smiled back. Leaning back in his seat, he closed his eyes in contentment. Yes, things were finally changing for the better.

CRASH!!!

And then, they suddenly took another unexpected turn.

About the Author

Morgan Lomax is a Christian and an Abeka Academy homeschool graduate. Ever since middle school, she has had a fervor for writing. Now she is a student at Truett McConnell University in Cleveland, Georgia and is working on her B.A. in English with a concentration in Creative Writing and two minors: Music and the Great Commission. She is also the pianist at West Hall Baptist Church in Oakwood, Georgia. When she is not writing or playing the piano, she enjoys drawing and spending time in nature. Currently, she lives in Georgia with her parents, dog, Sammie, and cat, Trapper. With everything she does, Morgan hopes to glorify God with the talents He has given her.

www.ingramcontent.com/pod-product-compliance
Lightning Source LLC
Chambersburg PA
CBHW061537210726
48287CB00006B/1993